Fanny Montgomery

The Bucklyn Shaig

A tale of the last century. Vol. 1

Fanny Montgomery

The Bucklyn Shaig
A tale of the last century. Vol. 1

ISBN/EAN: 9783337137823

Printed in Europe, USA, Canada, Australia, Japan

Cover: Foto ©Andreas Hilbeck / pixelio.de

More available books at **www.hansebooks.com**

THE BUCKLYN SHAIG.

A Tale of the last Century.

BY THE
HON. MRS. ALFRED MONTGOMERY,
AUTHOR OF "ASHTON HALL," POEMS, ETC.

" Vengeance is mine ; I will repay, saith the **Lord**."
Deut. xxxii. 35; *Romans* xii. 19 ; *Hebrews* x. 30.

IN TWO VOLUMES.—VOL. I.

LONDON:
RICHARD BENTLEY, 8, NEW BURLINGTON STREET,
Publisher in Ordinary to Her Majesty.
1865.

LONDON: PRINTED BY WILLIAM CLOWES AND SONS, STAMFORD STREET
AND CHARING CROSS.

DEDICATION.

THESE VOLUMES ARE DEDICATED

To the beloved memory of a near relative,
in whose dear society the Author first
visited the scenes in which this story is
laid; and to whom, half in jest, more than
twenty years ago, the promise was given
of writing a romance that should illustrate
them.

Hers was a mind in which the freshness
of youth continued undiminished by ad-
vancing years, and the purity and delicacy
of her superior nature remained untarnished
by the world. She possessed a depth of
thought, and a versatility of talent, which

were only equalled by her exquisite mo-
desty.

Wise, and yet tender; gentle, yet firm;
she was the TRUEST OF WOMEN, and THE
MOST FAITHFUL OF FRIENDS.

Her sweet face was the reflex of her soul.
The grave has closed over all; but the
remembrance can never perish. " Le passé
n'est pas mort; il n'est qu'absent."

IFIELD LODGE, CRAWLEY,
    August 8, 1865.

CONTENTS.

VOL. I.

CHAPTER VIII.

CHAPTER IX.

CHAPTER X.

CHAPTER XI.

CHAPTER XII.

THE BUCKLYN SHAIG.

CHAPTER I.

EARLY DAYS AND FIRST LOVE.

MANY years ago, near the eastern coast of
England, there stood (and there still stand),
on the opposite shores of a wood-encircled
lake, two wealthy mansions, the property
of two brothers.

Nutley Hall belonged to the representa-
tive of the elder branch of the family of
Baron Clifford. It stood in a wide park-
like domain, raised a little above the low
shore of the lake, which reflected its image
on its bosom, and surrounded and almost
embedded in magnificent trees.

There was something melancholy about

the old place, in spite of the well-tended gardens, and the southern sun streaming on the lichen-covered walls. It was a silent spot, buried in wood, glooming over the deep waters of the lake, and enlivened by few sounds beyond the warbling of the forest birds, or the occasional scream of the wild swans.

The trees had been cleared away near the water, and when the long line of golden light from the setting sun changed into pale yellow, and died off in paler green, there might often be seen the silent heron standing on one leg, by the side of a mossy stone, and gazing with unwearied patience into the still waters, watching motionless for his prey. Or, in the hot noontide, with a shrill cry, the wildfowl would rise from the surface of the lake, and wrinkling its placid face into countless eddies by the sweep of their wings, traverse it for several yards, and then drop silently and simultaneously upon its bosom.

There was little to break the monotony of wood and water, but here and there you caught a glimpse of a low range of hills in the distance, and on the other side of the walled-in road, which dammed the waters at the head of the lake, rose a grassy mound, surmounted by the ruins of an old tower, formerly a fortress belonging to the baron's family in wilder times than those of the Lord Clifford of our story.

In somewhat striking contrast with this wild and sylvan spot, was the scene of intense refinement and domestic peace which struck the spectator's eye on the other side of the deep haw-haw that divided the garden from the park. Beneath the spreading boughs of a huge cedar was a group that Watteau might have painted, only that there was more of family feeling and less of worldly effect than is usually found in the works of that artist.

Reclining on a long low couch was a lady, from whose sweet, earnest face the gradual approaches of a fatal disease had failed to efface the original beauty. The thick masses of raven hair seemed like an ebony frame to the white ivory of her forehead ; and beneath that placid brow lay the deep eyes that had not yet lost their Italian lustre beneath England's grey skies.

Angela, Lord Clifford's wife, was a relation of the princely house of Orsini, who, having been left an orphan while still very young, had been educated by the late Princess Orsini with her own children. She had married Lord Clifford in Rome, where his great wealth, and the common faith of the two families, had been motives cogent enough to induce Angela's relatives to put aside the objections arising from the immense distance (in those days, when railways and steam-boats were unknown) of the country to which their adopted daughter was to be exiled.

The present Princess Orsini, seated in an arm-chair opposite Angela, was the wife of the young Duke of Orsini, with whom Angela had been brought up, and had learnt to love almost as an elder brother, although the real relationship was but a distant one. The princess was a woman of about thirty, French by birth, and with much more liveliness of manners, but with less beauty of person, than her Italian friend. She held in her hand a piece of embroidery, and her busy fingers moved deftly, without the occupation interrupting her conversation.

At a little distance from the two ladies, and seated close to the haw-haw, with their feet hanging over the wall, were a lovely boy and girl. Rose Clifford, in hair and complexion was a true Saxon maiden, but in strange contrast with her fair skin and golden hair she had got her mother's deep Italian eyes.

Andrea Orsini was the very picture of a Roman boy : brown skin of the finest grain, and yet not brown, but rather golden ; dark locks, that at their tips had caught and imprisoned the rays of the sun ; red, full lips, and teeth made for laughter. Such was the infant heir of the house of Orsini.

As little Rose Clifford was slightly nervous at having to share Andrea's favourite position of sitting on the wall of the haw-

haw, she could only be induced to do so by Andrea's keeping his arm round her waist as a protection ; and while in this attitude the children were overheard by their parents in earnest conversation.

" Rosy, darling, I don't understand how it is that in your house, though it is so large and beautiful, you have no statue of Our Lady on the staircase, with a lamp burning before it. Why, Rosy, in the Orsini Palace, at Rome, there is one on every landing. And there is always one in all the houses, particularly in a house like ours."

" Well, Andy, dear, you know the fact is, this country is not Catholic ; and it is not very long ago that we used to be afraid (so papa has told me), even to have a pries in our house, or to have mass. So that is why, Andy, we do not put sacred objects much about the house. But you know in mamma's room and in mine we are not afraid, and there are plenty there."

" I tell you what it is," said Andrea, looking grave, " I do not like you living in a country where people are afraid to do what they like in our holy religion. You know, Rosy, you are to come away with me, and be my wife in the Orsini Palace, and I think the sooner we settle about it the better. This England is not the place for us, I shall carry you away with me."

These last words were said with a toss of the rich dark curls, and a flash from those beautiful eyes, that made Rosy almost feel as if Andrea were angry. Her little cheeks turned crimson, and she said very gravely,

" I think, Andrea, we had better not talk about that; and, besides, I love my own country in spite of all you say."

Andrea drew his arm tighter round Rosy's waist, and turning his face full upon her, said,

" But you *will*, Rosy, be my wife : you know you must, Rosy ; it is all settled, and I will not have any wife but you———."

Rosy's hand began to push away that of the little boy that was clinging closer round her, and with affronted dignity she replied—

" Please, Andrea, say nothing more

about it, and let us talk of something else."

With one bound Andrea had quitted his companion, even at the risk of pushing Rosy off her insecure seat into the haw-haw; and, scarlet with emotion, and with tears in his eyes, he rushed away to his mother's side.

" Mamma mia," he exclaimed, " Rosy says she will not be my wife, she will not leave this horrid England, she will not come to the Palazzo Orsini. But she *will*, will she not? For you know, mamma mia, I must marry Rosy; I cannot live without her."

The last words were said in softer tones, and with a burst of tears the little head was hid in his mother's arms.

Lady Clifford looked towards Rosy sitting on the edge of the haw-haw, and perceived that she, too, was overcome with emotion; but in her case it was from terror, and, springing up to her rescue, Lady Clifford lifted the child from the ground, and gently asked what it all meant.

The Princess Orsini, well used to Andrea's

passionate bursts of feeling, was calmly soothing her little son, and kissing away the big tears.

" Dear Andrea, you must not tease Rosy by asking her to promise you things which cannot happen for many years. You must be gentle and kind to her, and so make her love you ; and it will be quite soon enough to talk about her being your wife in ten years' time, for you know you are now only eleven."

" But do you think *then*, mamma mia, Rosy will leave this England, where the sky is never blue, and the sun never hot, and come to our dear Italy with me ?"

" I hope so, my darling child," responded the princess, with a smile. " But say no more about it to her just now. You can talk to me about it whenever you please, but you will only frighten poor Rosy if you are so violent."

Lady Clifford, meanwhile, was reassuring Rosy ; and as the little girl was very fond of her young friend, and had no other objec-tion to these childish notions about becom-

ing the future Princess Orsini than arose
from a slight maidenly reserve, and a feeling
that Andrea was rather pushing, she was
very ready to be kissed and make it up, and
then both the little lovers, hand in hand,
were sent on a run down the broad garden-
walk, to meet Father Netherby and Padre
Tomaso, who were returning from the
village.

When the ladies had regained their seats,
after this brief episode, Lady Clifford looked
silently, but with a smile, full into the princess's face. Their eyes met, and both laughed
out at the amusing scene of Andrea's vehe-
mence about his little sweetheart, who was
only ten and a half, and, consequently, as
young to be affianced as he was to be thinking of such matters.

" Do you really think, Louise," said Lady
Clifford to the princess, " that we shall ever
succeed in bringing about this alliance,
which our children seem to have as much at
heart as their mothers ?   Are you sure the
prince wishes it as much as you do?"

" Oh! Alfonso desires nothing more,"

replied the princess. " It was only the other day when he and your husband were coming down to the door, where the carriage was waiting, in Paris, to take us to the coast, that he said to me, ' Do what you can, carissima, to enlist Angela in our cause, and I, meanwhile, will talk to Clifford.' "

Angela sat silent for a few moments, her eyes fixed on the western sky, where the orange glories of the sunset were becoming streaked with deep red as the sun sank behind the trees ; then, without looking at the princess, she said—

" You may imagine, dear Louise, that, were the case reversed, and that I gave a daughter of mine, born and nurtured in Italy, to be exiled into this cold country, where we, with our faith and our politics, nearly always have to suffer ; and that your son were English, I could not do it. You understand me, dear. My own fate has not been an unhappy one. No woman with such a husband as dear George has been to me can ever have a right to complain. But still, look at what England has done for me! At most I may expect to see two more winters, and then the chill that has passed from these grey mists into my Italian blood, that had been fed by the richest sunlight, will have done its work, and little Rosy will be an orphan."

"Dear Angela, I cannot bear to hear you say it. My dearest, you are better: I see an improvement even since I came. You will soon regain your strength."

"You see an improvement, Louise, because we are now enjoying our brief English summer. But when this mass of forest land lays down its green and brown vesture on the damp earth, and that great lake sends up its clammy mists and enters the house, and creeps into my window, and catches my breath, like the foretaste of the tomb, then my cough will return, and I shall continue to get weaker and thinner. No, Louise, dear, I must not shut my eyes to the truth—nor yours—because you will help me to meet that death I have long ceased to dread. But I must keep it from

George as long as possible, for I think it would break his heart."

" Does he suspect, Angela, how ill you think yourself ?"

Lady Clifford paused before replying, and then said—

."" I cannot tell, Louise. Sometimes I think he does. He talks of taking me to Rome this winter. I wish it were possible, Louise. I must tell you what I dread," exclaimed Lady Clifford, as she bent forwards, and laying her hand on the princess' arm, made her drop her work and look up. " If I die, and dear George follows me before Rose is married, or is of age, I fear —I dread—he will appoint her uncle, Roger Clifford, to be her guardian. Louise," she said, dropping her voice, and doubling her pressure on her relative's arm, " *I detest that man !*"

" Why is it, Angela, you shrink so from him ?" replied the princess, with a slight tone in her voice as if Angela's feelings seemed to her without just ground. " I hope you are not going to tell me he has the 'evil eye.' You know I am French, cannot adopt all your Italian superstitions about that."

" Whether he has the evil eye or not, I neither know nor care. But I am sure he has a very sinister dark nature, and I fear that in his heart he has renounced the Faith."

" Oh, Angela, impossible !"

" Listen, Louise! I have told you I do not believe I have many years to live; can you think that, with that thought ever before me, I would dare to speak against Roger Clifford, were it not that my convictions on the subject are so strong that I feel I ought, as a duty to my child, to communicate them to you, and through you to Alfonso in my child's interest ?"

" If your suppositions be correct, Angela," said the princess, " how dreadful for these two motherless children of his !" How old are they now ?"

" Teresa is rather more than thirteen, and a most interesting child. She is at a convent school in Paris. Her father talks of having her home, but I trust she will, for the present, be left where she is. Robert is much older; he was seventeen his last birthday, and is left also in Paris, with a tutor."

" Have you spoken to George of this?" said the princess.

" I have tried, but it is impossible. He thinks I am prejudiced. And you know, dear Louise, the very fact of my being a foreigner makes me doubly afraid of shocking my dear husband's feelings about any of his family ; or seeming to misunderstand the character of those around me. I would not do so even to you were it not for Rose's sake. I wish you were likely yourself to see enough of Roger Clifford to judge of him. You would feel as I do, and, like me, you would be tempted to believe at least some of the dark stories of his gambling and profligate habits when he is abroad. You are aware that he is scarcely ever at Raymond Castle."

" Will he be there before 1 leave ?"

" I think it probable. He told George

that he would find him here on his return
from Paris."

"Angela, does he know that George and
Alfonso have gone to Vienna?   If what
you say be true, if, in short, supposing your
doubts about the unhappy man's faith to
have any foundation, it would be dreadful
for him to guess, or in any way to arrive at
the fact that your husband and mine are
gone on a secret mission from Rome to the
Prince.   If it be true that Roger has embraced the religion of the state, he can only
have done so to curry favour with the House
of Hanover, and from that moment he
becomes a dangerous neighbour to us."

"I do not think there is any fear of that,
for I believe Roger to be now on his way
back from Spain; consequently they will not
cross each other's path.   And when they
all return, there can be no occasion for
saying more than that after seeing you and
Andrea safe on your way to the coast, our
husbands remained for a time in Paris.
This journey to Vienna is known only to us
two."

" Thank God for that !" exclaimed Louise. " But when our husbands are returned, I should rather like, Angela, to meet Roger here. I might be of use in aiding you to some more decided convictions one way or the other. If I judge him differently from you it will be a relief to you to be encouraged in changing your opinion. If I, too, think him bad and false, surely we ought to warn George not to place confidence in one who may betray us. But all this while, dear Angela," continued the princess, trying to brighten up herself, and to cheer her friend, " I do not know why we should suppose that even, dearest—which God forbid !—you are taken away early to the world of rest and peace, we should think George is not to live to see Rose married, and a mother."

" Neither can I say, Louisa, why I should think so. But love sometimes seems to endow us with something of the spirit of prophecy. It foresees what it dreads. It divines what it cannot know. You always told me I was too imaginative. When I was in Italy, in my girlhood, I never knew what apprehension was. Whether it be that this silent land, this dear sad home of my adoption, has imparted some of its seriousness to my nature, I cannot tell; but certainly of late years I seem to have developed in myself a strange faculty of guessing—almost knowing—what *will* be. Perhaps it is all fancy. Perhaps, Louise, it is the shadow of the future world, falling like light upon the present life, and enabling me to see more clearly. For, dear Louise, the shadows of heaven are brighter than the noonday of this world."

The princess bent forward to kiss the beautiful face of the speaker, that was lighted up with the enthusiasm of her southern nature. The tears were in her eyes as she said :

" Angela, I will not gainsay you. I love you too dearly to bear to think of losing you; I would tie your wings if I could. As it is, I can only pray to God to spare you to us yet, and entreat you to do all you can to preserve your invaluable health, and to consent to live."

Angela raised her eyes to the red disc of the evening sun. The great globe seemed to quiver as she gazed upon it through her tears, and she murmured, "God's dear will be done." The sun sank behind the forest, and the blue mists of evening fell like a shroud over the landscape.

CHAPTER II.

THE HALL AND THE CASTLE.

RAYMOND CASTLE, the property of Roger Clifford, could be seen from the windows of Nutley Hall when autumn left. the trees bare; and from one part of the park its tower and broad frontage was full in view, so that when Angela had first married and come to England, she had been in the habit of establishing a variety of signals with her sister-in-law, Mrs. Clifford, by means of a flagstaff and coloured flags, with reference to their arrangements for meeting and riding together in the course of each day.

This, perhaps, had been the happiest

portion of Angela's married life, although she was not yet blessed with the little rosebud now unfolding beneath her care ; for Angela had been married eight years before her only child was born. But at the period of which we speak, she was still in the enjoyment of the health and spirits of youth, and spite of the difficulties of travelling in those days, her devoted husband had generally succeeded in taking her to Italy to breathe her native air at least every third winter. On one of these occasions Mrs. Clifford had accompanied Angela ; and it was there that her second child, a girl, was prematurely born, and the young mother died in her confinement.

Roger Clifford had not accompanied his wife. The then dissolute court in Paris, where his high connections and his love of play procured him free access, had greater attractions for Roger than travelling through Italy with a wife in delicate health, and whose tastes were the very opposite to his own.

Angela had nursed her sister-in-law with

devoted affection, and as it was in the old feudal castle of Bracciano * that Mrs. Clifford had given birth to the little Teresa, it was near the shores of a lake far wilder than that of her married home, that the young wife and mother lay buried. Her life would have been a very unhappy one, had it not been that the sweetness and brightness of her nature seemed to carry her unscathed through the sharpest sorrows. She bore her husband's constant neglect with such unalterable calm, that sometimes Angela's hot Italian nature found it difficult not to be angry with the English woman's passive endurance. But when Mildred would perceive the flush of anger glowing through the clear, dead white of Angela's foreign complexion, she would gently slide up to her sister-in-law, and whisper with a smile and a tear:

" I should have no cross if I had not

* The castle of Bracciano was built by the Orsini. They sold it, towards the close of the eighteenth century, to the Odescalchis, in whose possession it was when the author visited it. Since then it has again changed hands.

this; and if I had no cross here, how could I hope for a happy death?"

"Oh, Mildred!" Angela would exclaim, "you are always talking of death. Give *me* life—life with its crown of gold—life with its ringing laugh, and its buoyant step, and its hand full of flowers—tranquil and pure, but joyous and hopeful. No, Mildred, I cannot understand you. I feel I must *live* before I die—I must taste and know all life is, and gives."

"Ah, Angela! it were better to die," Mildred replied, "before the drop of intolerable bitterness had fallen into the cup of life: it were better to die than live to exclaim in a moment of temptation, 'I cannot bear more!' This will hardly happen to you, Angela; it might, you know, to me." And now changing her tone, she said, "Will you put on your hat and come out with me? I am going to the Capuchin Convent half an hour before the Ave Maria, and that will do both of us more good than all you and I are likely to say about life and death!"

In this way Angela would perceive that her English sister-in-law's heroic patience sprang from a better source than indifference; but while she loved Mildred more, she grew in detestation of Roger Clifford.

Mildred Clifford's death was the first severe sorrow Angela had ever known, and it told greatly on her character, for while it threw a shade of sadness over her impetuous nature, it called forth greater depths of tenderness than she had ever yet evinced.

Roger Clifford was summoned from Paris by the sad news; but he did not reach Bracciano till long after the remains of his young wife were laid in the family vault, in a chapel built by the Orsinis in the Capuchin Church.

Roger was quiet, grave, and respectable in his grief ; and when Angela complained to her husband that he seemed to feel less than might have been expected, Lord Clifford was always ready with excuses and explanations ; and assured Angela that his brother was one of those who feel things deeply and long, though making little outward show of grief.

The little infant had been christened Teresa by the dying mother's special request. "She will need courage in the life that lies before her, and therefore I put her under the special protection of that great saint and courageous woman."

Little Robert Clifford had been left at Raymond Castle under the care of a distant female relative, who went to take up her abode there during Mr. and Mrs. Clifford's absence.

Angela devoted herself absorbingly to the care of the little infant, and it was in watching the motherless babe that she first felt the intensity of desire to become a mother herself.

As soon as the breath of spring was filled with the perfume of the blue violets that fringed the lake of Bracciano, it was decided that Lord and Lady Clifford should return to England, taking with them the little Teresa.

Both Angela and her husband acutely

felt the sadness of leaving the tomb of the poor English lady, who lay so far away from her own land and her own people; and Lord Clifford had even suggested to Roger that the body should be removed to the family vault at Nutley; but Roger had replied that his nerves would not bear the anxiety of fancying the many accidents that might befall the sacred deposit in so long and perilous a journey.

Angela was inclined to be doubtful of the sincerity of this reply, but she did not venture to contest it, and she soothed her grief by occupying herself, with Roger's authority, in choosing the designs and superintending the execution of a beautiful monument to the memory of her friend.

When Lord and Lady Clifford returned to Nutley, they were greatly in hope that Roger would settle quietly at Raymond Castle, and content himself with the society of his family and the care of his children; but this was not the case.

Although Raymond Castle was by far the finest house of the two, the estate and property connected with it was less than one-fourth in value to that attached to Nutley Hall, and belonging to the elder brother.

Roger was an ambitious man, and it was easy enough for any one less attached to him than Lord Clifford to perceive that it was jealousy of his elder brother that kept him so constantly absent from his own estate. During, however, the first few months of his widowhood he seemed to consider it his duty to remain at home, and it was then that Angela first had full opportunity of studying the character of her brother-in-law. There was a mysterious charm in his manner which fascinated most persons, although on Angela it seemed to produce the contrary effect. He was very different from his elder brother, and the difference was increased by his having lived a great deal abroad, and contracted something foreign in his habits and appearance.

Lord Clifford had a frank, fair countenance, with a clear blue eye, and auburn hair. His complexion was almost too delicate for a man, and there was apt to be a hectic colour in his cheeks. He was extremely graceful, but perhaps he was too delicately formed for the perfection of manly beauty. His health had never been strong, but yet he was a thorough Englishman in his love of sport, and was passionately attached to his country and his home.

Roger was taller and darker than his brother, and looked older. He had long almond-shaped, deep-set eyes, a dark pencilled brow, slightly arched. His lips were delicately cut, but thin and flexible; and sometimes he wore a fixed smile, not in harmony with the rest of his expression, and with the stern keenness of his eye. Angela would often speak of it as " that cruel smile," and said that it froze her blood. Roger was a musician, and had an exquisite voice. He was an accomplished scholar, and spoke French, Italian, and Spanish equally well. His tastes were expensive, and he would say that unless he could afford to fit up his gloomy old castle after his own fancy, and fill it with guests, he never would long reside there.

No one, however, but its discontented master thought Raymond Castle gloomy. It stood on high ground, overlooking the forest lands, in the centre of which Nutley Hall lay buried, and commanding the whole range of those blue hills but barely visible between the trees at the latter place.

The park was large, and beautifully laid out, with a great expanse of green sward in front of the castle, sloping down to several small ponds gleaming in the sunshine, like islets of silver. Beyond that was woodland and hill, and long lines of purple distance to the west. Near the castle was a group of tall Scotch firs, bending a little out of the perpendicular, and standing like sentinels alone on the place. Further down the slope were magnificent oaks, elms, and chestnuts, silver fir, and birch. Through a hanging wood to the north lay two wide paths, purposely cut through the thicket to admit of the view of the hills beyond.

The road wound from the house down-
hill, past the small fish ponds, and through
groups of trees to the lodge gate out into
the high-road, which to the north led to
the village of Nutley, and to the south to
the market town of Blackdean.

The castle entrance was beneath the great
clock-tower, through Norman arches; and
as you stood just outside the tower at the
east, the park, and wood and hills, and the
Scotch firs standing with red stems against
the western sky, formed as lovely a picture,
framed by the stonework of the arch, as it
was possible to imagine.

In Nutley Hall there was a chapel at the
top of the house, which had been used in
the time of the persecution of the Catholics.
This chapel was panelled with dark oak
rather more than half-way up the walls,
and behind the altar was a sliding panel,
known only to Lord Clifford and a few of
the old domestics, where in former days the
priest not unfrequently lay concealed in
the rare occasions when he had been able,
in disguise and through many perils, to

come and administer the sacraments and consolations of the faith to the present baron's not very distant ancestors.

There once had been a chapel at Raymond Castle also, but it had been long disused, and now served only as a lumber-room, or as a studio to an Italian artist, who sometimes accompanied Roger Clifford on his return from the Continent for a few summer months at the castle. Mrs. Clifford had had a small oratory fitted up for her own use; and Teresa's old nurse, Mrs. Dorothy, had always kept it in good order and well dusted, " for the dear child," she would say, " when she shall be old enough to know the blessings of her mother's faith." The other servants would sometimes remonstrate with Mrs. Dorothy, as she was generally called, that she spoke as if the mother's faith were not the father's also.

Mrs. Dorothy never made any reply, but a close observer would see that on those occasions she slightly compressed her lips.

One thing was certain. It was Roger himself who had done away with the chapel, and had, as he said for the greater convenience of others, removed the whole furniture to a room at the top of a small house in the village. You might have passed it a hundred times and never have guessed that behind those very ordinary-looking windows, in that modest-looking white house, not much bigger than a cottage, there crept, Sundays and feast-days, throughout the year, a quiet group of devout followers of the faith of their forefathers.

The priest lived in the lower part of the house, and, at the time of our story, was a Jesuit father, the Father Netherby that we have already heard of as coming from the village, with Andrew Orsini's Italian tutor and chaplain to the family, Padre Tomaso.

Shortly after his wife's death, Roger decided on breaking up his establishment at Raymond Castle, and sending little Robert, then about eight years old, to school.

Lord Clifford, as well as Angela, had been much disturbed by this arrangement, and had entreated Roger to let his son be entrusted to their care, as well as Teresa.

Roger had been profuse in his expressions of gratitude, but firm in his refusal. He had put it on the pretext that his son being heir to a very much smaller property than that of Nutley Hall, he would not have him brought up in such magnificence.

"Moreover," added he, "Lady Clifford will have sons of her own, and at least my boy shall be the heir in the house where he is educated. I am too thankful for Angela's offer about my poor little girl. I could not leave her in better hands. And it is not of the same importance for her, at least for the next few years, as she never can be a personage of much consideration in either house."

Roger therefore sent off his son and heir to a distance, and from thence he was transmitted to a school in Paris; and thus, with the exception of a few brief weeks, he was never at Castle Raymond till his education was completed.

Meanwhile Angela, with the aid of Mrs. Dorothy, who was engaged as nurse as soon as the family returned from Italy after Mrs.

Clifford's death, devoted herself entirely to the care of the little Teresa. A more engaging child could hardly be found. To strangers she was grave and silent, but with Aunt Angela she was all bright intelligence. Thoughtful beyond her years, she had shown a tendency to love study and reflection before she was seven years of age. She had inherited her father's eyes and thoughtful brow, but the sweetness of the lower part of the face was her mother's gift. She was only three years and a half when Lord and Lady Clifford were blest by the birth of little Rose. She was born in June, and from the first moment of her life, unlike most babies, had so lovely a complexion, that when brought to her mother's bed-side that she might see the little creature of a night old, and say what name she was to receive in baptism that day, Angela had at once decided she should be called Rose.

Teresa soon began to patronize her infant cousin, and as they grew together nothing could be prettier than the contrast between these lovely children. They went by the

name of " Night and Day "—Teresa with
eyes like deep night, and Rose with hair
like Aurora.

Angela undertook for a long time their
education. She taught the little maidens to
read, and to work, and to talk Italian. But
when Rose was five years old and Teresa
eight, she engaged a French lady as their
governess, and the work of education grew
for a short time more serious under the
care of Madame de Bray.

This, however, continued only till Teresa
was nine years old. And then one day
Angela received a letter from Roger Clifford which caused her the greatest anxiety
and pain. It was dated from Florence,
and after describing to her in his clever
style the amusements of the carnival, which
was just closing, it went on to say :

" And now, my dear sister-in-law, I have
a task to perform, the first part of which is
simply impossible, and the second painful.
I have to express my gratitude for your
unwearied care of my little daughter. When
you took her you had no child of your own

to occupy your time and your affections. I thought your kindness immense even then, and I have lived in astonishment ever since the birth of your own daughter at your continuing your hospitality and your care to my poor child. But while I can never thank you enough for what you have done, I should be wrong in asking, nay, even in allowing, you to continue this favour.

" Your little Rose (is not that her name ?) is born to bloom in richer lands than my poor dark flower, and I should be doing my child an injustice in allowing her, just at the period when impressions are the strongest, to be brought up surrounded by the luxury of Nutley Hall. The same motives which actuated me in the course I thought it right to pursue with regard to Robert, are doubly cogent in the case of Teresa, who can never have but the poor pittance of a younger child's portion, enough, and only enough, to pay her dot in some convent, which no doubt will be the best and safest career for her, if career it can be called.

" Since it is for this I destine her (and I

believe I am rigorously carrying out by this resolve her poor mother's wishes), it is much better that Teresa should complete her education in a religious house, such as we may easily select for her in Paris. And let us hope that beginning so young to habituate her mind to the gentle routine of convent life she will never have any other (I won't shock you, dear Angela, by saying any higher) aspirations; and that thus she will dispose of herself happily for life, and certainly, also, so far usefully that it will prevent the necessity of my taking from Robert's future fortune more than the modest sum required to secure her admission in some house of the Carmelites (I say Carmelites only because of her name, and from a notion I have that her mother wished it—you know how very devout poor Mildred was). If it is not asking too much of you, Angela, I think I had rather leave the choice of the convent to you.

" George writes me, he hopes to take you to Rome this autumn. Carry little Teresa with you as far as Paris, and locate her there as you think best. I have written by the same post to my agent, to desire him to enter into any arrangements my brother may acquaint him with respecting the payment of the pension.

" Excuse all the additional trouble I am giving you, dear Angela. The child has seen nothing of me, and therefore will not feel a separation, which will hardly be increased by this arrangement. She will suffer parting from you, but it will only be a judicious commencement of that life of negation which, as a nun, she will always lead.

" Once more, a thousand thanks, dear sister. Teresa will, I hope, always be grateful to you and George.

" By the by, I bring you, on my return, the most exquisite rosary of highly-wrought gold beads, with a cross set in rubies at the end, that I ever beheld. They say it originally belonged to her late majesty, Mary of Modena—an additional reason for its finding favour in your eyes, my loyal sister.

" Yours affectionately,

" ROGER CLIFFORD."

No words could express Angela's feelings on reading this letter. She thought it utterly heartless towards the child, and ungrateful towards her and her husband. She would have rejoiced if later on, when old enough to think for herself, the little Teresa had elected to enter religion. And, indeed, with Angela's opinion of her father's character, it seemed to her the best and happiest lot for the poor girl; but Roger's scheming about it shocked her inexpressibly.

Lord Clifford was one of those amiable, easy men who take no strong views on any subject (devotion to the house of Stuart and to the Catholic faith apart), and therefore he tried to argue with his wife that, on the whole, Roger's conduct was right and natural.

"You know, Angela," he would say, "Roger has very deep feelings beneath all that affected indifference. Unhappily, his susceptibility has rendered him jealous, and though I believe firmly in his affection for me, yet I have always felt it was a misfortune that the two estates should be so close together. It causes him always to be

reverting in a painful way to his lesser
fortune. And certainly nature made a mistake. Roger is ambitious, and ought to
have been the elder brother. I am a plain
man, and am content to pass my days in
seclusion with my Angel and my Rosebud.
But though I cannot feel with Roger, and
am almost inclined to be angry with him
for robbing us of little Teresa, yet I honour
the firmness of his purpose and the decision
of his character. Possibly this may arise
from my being myself of so much more
malleable material. But then you know, dear
Angela, I have you to enact all the fire and
the force, and so save me the trouble."

Thus, half in jest and half in earnest,
Lord Clifford strove to console his wife for
her disappointment, and to protect Roger
from her severe judgment. He did not
succeed ; but Angela kept her thoughts to
herself. And the end of it was, that little
Teresa accompanied them to Paris on their
way to Italy, and was left there at a convent of Ursuline nuns. Rose and Madame
de Bray went with them to Rome, and

Mrs. Dorothy went as Angela's maid. They passed the winter there, and there it was that Angela began to feel that the English climate had been making secret, and till then unsuspected, ravages on her constitution.

They did not return to Nutley Hall for nearly two years, and it was the end of June that the opening scene of our story took place, the family·having arrived in April. Roger was coming home. It was whispered that heavy losses at play made it necessary that he should keep very quiet for a time, and he talked of bringing back Teresa from Paris with him. Angela feared her father's household would hardly be conducted in a way to make it a desirable residence for a young girl. Lord Clifford had not heard the rumours about the motives for his brother's return, and if he had would not have believed them. He was rejoiced to think that he should again enjoy his companionship, and he thought nothing more right and natural than that, intending to remain at home, he should bring back Teresa with him.

Lord Clifford, on his arrival in England, had found business of the greatest importance to the Royalist cause awaiting his decision and advice. Nothing could be done without an interview with the Pretender, then at Vienna. As soon, therefore, as he had seen Angela and Rose safely settled at home, he had returned to Paris to meet the Orsinis, who had promised to follow them very shortly from Rome, and spend the summer in England. When he did so, it was thought better, for many reasons, that the princess and Andrea should continue their journey with the domestic chaplain and their rather large retinue of servants, alone, and that the prince, who was a personal friend of the Pretender, should accompany Lord Clifford to Vienna.

Their return was now hourly expected, and as Roger had written word that he, too, was coming home, the hall and the castle were likely soon to be enlivened by the presence of the two families.

CHAPTER III.

DOMESTIC.

ABOUT a week had passed since the scene in the garden between Rose and Andrea, when Lady Clifford and the princess were sitting, late in the day, by the open window. The air was sultry and oppressive, as if it foreboded a storm. Angela had been talking with her friend of their mutual relations and acquaintances in France and Italy. The children were playing in the next room, with the door open into that where the ladies were sitting, when they all heard the sound of a horse galloping up to the front door, and the bell ring violently. Angela blushed and then turned pale. Every hour she and the princess expected to hear of their husbands' return, and Angela hoped this might be a messenger from them. The princess, knowing how easily Lady Clifford was agitated in her then delicate health, tried to make her continue the conversation till they could know what the ring at the bell meant. Presently a servant entered, and said:

"My lady, there is a messenger come from Mr. Clifford in London. He has brought this letter, and says his master is on his way."

Angela broke the seal, and read aloud:

"My dear Sister-in-law,

"I arrived from Paris three days ago, bringing Teresa with me. I had written, as perhaps you have heard, to the castle, to have everything in readiness for our arrival; but Teresa seems so unwell that I am anxious to see her at once safe at the end of her journey. I hope, this being the case, you will not think me intruding if I bring her to you until her own home is ready.

"I am a bad hand at having the care of children, and I do not quite know what to think of the two big black eyes and unnaturally sad, pale face that I see now in the arm-chair before me.

"I send a man on horseback at once. We cannot arrive till late in the evening.

"Yours, with many apologies,

"ROGER CLIFFORD."

"Louise," said Angela, looking up with a bright smile, "this is a most happy providence. I shall have that dear child here, and once I have got her, I will keep her."

In a few moments the whole house was in motion preparing for the reception of the welcome guests, and the door of the great hall was opened while the carriage was still climbing the slope.

First, was lifted out by the old butler, a little pale girl, in a dark blue frock and a black bonnet, who said instantly, but very quietly, in a decided voice :

"Put me down, if you please."

Angela caught her in her arms, and Rose flung hers round her. The little creature seem pleased, but half frightened ; but she returned Rose's embrace eagerly. Roger, looking more of a foreigner than ever, stepped forward with a number of cold and graceful apologies for their arriving so suddenly, and hoped his doing so would not inconvenience Angela.

"Why, Roger, we are delighted to have you, of course," she exclaimed, warmly, forgetting, in her natural hospitality, the aversion she had to him, or, perhaps, not feeling it in the presence of little Teresa, who was as her own adopted child. "We cannot let you go to the castle to-night. Nothing there is ready for you; besides, you must remain at least a few days till we see how Teresa gets on. You would be anxious about her up there all by yourself."

He acquiesced so courteously, that the princess, already much struck by his appearance, began to think all Angela had said about him was the effect of imagination.

It was settled he should stop at Nutley Hall.

Nothing could be happier and more peaceful than the family circle, completed and assembled at Nutley Hall a few days after the arrival of Roger.

Teresa soon recovered her looks and her strength under the careful nursing she received. Lord Clifford and the Prince Orsini joined them very shortly, and though they both were at first slightly depressed by the ill success of their expedition; and of their losses in the Jacobite cause, still the repose of home, and the presence around them of all they held most dear, rendered it impossible for all parties not to feel that the " lines had fallen to them in goodly places."

Angela's health was considerably improved. She could join in the walks they took of an afternoon ; she could accompany Roger and the prince in their singing in the evening. She was an admirable musician, and had a rich contralto voice. The prince also was considered, even in Italy, as being an excellent performer, and his voice was magnificent. The princess appreciated, though she could not contribute, and so while the above-named trio were performing, she and Madame de Bray used to whisper French together, and talk of their beloved country and gay Paris, while Lord Clifford sat enjoying the music, and never missing a single note, like a silent Englishman as he was.

Madame de Bray was born of a noble family, though compelled by misfortune to employ her talents in education. She and the princess were intimate with many persons of the same circle of society, and Madame de Bray, in happier times, had been at the French Court.

The strong feeling that Angela had expressed with regard to Roger, seemed to soften down under the influence of his polished manners and the charm of his conversation. He seldom spoke of politics, still less of religion; and it seemed impossible not to feel the trust in him that an honest man and a gentleman inspires; or at least one whom we believe to be such, because he looks and speaks like one.

The princess did not hesitate to take Madame de Bray into her confidence with regard to Andrea and Rose. She would say to her :

"You know, my dear madame, Lady Clifford's health is so delicate, that I cannot conceal from myself the too great probability of her not living to see dear Rose married. Lord Clifford is a most amiable and excellent man, I have the greatest affection for him ; but I doubt his being a man of much independence of character. And now really, between ourselves, I think I had better candidly tell you what I am afraid of. I tremble lest he should think it wise to marry Rose with her cousin Robert, and so unite the two properties ; for though of course it would involve all the difficulties of endeavouring to obtain the necessary dispensation for admitting of a marriage between cousins, yet considering how much may be said to hang upon it, and the great importance in this country of keeping up the good old Catholic families,

I cannot but think the permission would be obtained from the Holy See."

Madame de Bray looked a little grave, and replied :

" I should consider that a very undesirable alliance, my dear princess. At the same time, I quite foresee the possibility of the danger. Lord Clifford is extremely attached to his brother."

" Do tell me, madame, what sort of a boy is Robert ?"

" We have seen very little of him. I am told that he shows considerable talent. But he has been brought up entirely abroad, and is now at a German university."

" What ! a Protestant university. Impossible !"

" He is at Bonn ; and, as you are aware, he can there declare himself either Protestant or Catholic, or neither."

" And which *has* he done ?" asked the princess.

" I believe he has followed the third course, and adopted no religion at all. And I am afraid that is exactly what his father wished.

You know Mr. Clifford is a very ambitious man. Our faith is an impediment, absolute and entire, to his ever rising in this country. The House of Commons, and the court, and the bar, even had he ever thought of that, are absolutely closed to him. He cannot hold a commission in the army, or even exercise any influence in his own county as a magistrate. This is extremely galling to a man of his temper, and though he himself will, probably—whether from family pride, or, let us hope, from still having the faith though he does not live up to it—never openly renounce the Catholic Church, yet I am afraid he would not be sorry that his son, later on, by open apostacy, should become an eligible candidate for some of the honours and places the Court and the Government may have to bestow."

"But, dear madame, do you imagine Lord Clifford has any idea of the state of the case with regard to his brother's feelings?"

"I do not believe he has. Nor would it be easy to enlighten him on the subject.

He is devoted to his younger brother, and what with Mr. Clifford's being almost always absent abroad, and with ourselves going so often to Italy, added to Mr. Clifford's careful conduct when in his brother's house, I am not much surprised that he does not suspect the truth."

"I perceive, indeed," said the princess, "that Mr. Clifford seems to be bitten with some of the German philosophical views of the day, and to admire the lawless spirit which is unhappily gaining ground in our own France. But I own that in a man of the world, like Mr. Clifford, I had not attached much importance to this."

"There can be no doubt," rejoined Madame de Bray, "that Mr. Clifford has a great charm about him—a something that excites one's interest and curiosity. But if his son inherits his father's opinions, it would break my heart that he should become the husband of my darling Rose."

"But surely, madame, Angela might obtain a promise from her husband that Rose shall be affianced to Andrea. There can

be no reason why the question should not
be settled at once, if only Rose's parents can
be brought to desire it as much as the
prince and myself."

" Unfortunately, Lady Clifford is not
likely to have any influence with my lord
on that subject; I mean on the subject of
her feelings for his brother. He has
always shown a slight jealousy of Lady
Clifford's interference about any member of
his own family, and has seemed to be apprehensive that, not being an Englishwoman,
she will misunderstand his relatives, and
perhaps depreciate his country and customs.
It would, of course, be a noble and wealthy
alliance for Rose to become the wife of the
heir of the Orsinis. But then it obliterates
the heiress of the elder branch of the
Cliffords under the shadow of a great
Italian house. We must hope, dear princess, that the prayers of the martyred
priest, who was great uncle to the present
Lord Clifford, may prevail to bring about
what we desire."

" Then it is true, is it, that some of the

blood of the Cliffords has been shed for the faith ?"

"Quite true. He was the priest here, in this very place. You know in Queen Elizabeth's fatal reign, it was hanging matter to celebrate mass. Father Francis was just concluding the august sacrifice when he was seized in his vestments at the altar. There is preserved in the Chapel House at Nutley the letter he wrote the eve of his martyrdom. It is partly in cypher, but can easily be made out enough to perceive the sense. I happen to have a copy of the interesting document at this moment in my work-bag, for being desirous of sending it to my brother in France I asked Father Netherby to let me see it. Here it is :

" RIGHT REVEREND,

"I received your commands with all humility, and promptitude in execution, for I had taken possession of B. Paul's XX place about twenty hours before it came to me. Now I earnestly beg your prayers that I may constantly follow on to pursue the end of perseverance.

" Mr. Hood, I hope, will be able to make some little relation of what hath passed hitherto.

" All that I ask of any is that (which) Saint Andrew begged of the people, ' *ne impedient passionem,*' God's holy will be done *in æternum.*

" Your poor

" BROTHER FRANCIS.*

" *Nov.* 12."

" How proud Lord Clifford must be of having such noble examples in his family?"

" Yes, he is indeed, and proud too, of he ' Acts of Attainder,' which you may almost say form the principal family papers of this great house. Formerly half this

* The above, which was copied from the original IS., is authentic. The surname in the original is Bell. A few cyphers, not essential to the meaning, are omitted.

county, and nearly the whole of the next, belonged to the house of Clifford, besides the property in the north of England.   But one rich farm after another went, for every child that was known to have been baptized in the Catholic Church, or for the celebration of mass (when it was found out), or for having harboured a priest, or for the priest having been called to administer the last sacraments to 'the dying.   You may say that the archives of this family are so many claims to the palm of martyrdom, so many title-deeds to a higher place in the many mansions of our Father's kingdom. They count their riches, not by what they have gained, not by the rent-roll of their estates, but by their losses and their forfeitures in the cause of the faith!"

"But surely the sufferings of Catholics in this country are not what they were? They follow their faith without any actual danger now."

"That is true," replied madame; "nevertheless, what they call the 'Disability Bills' are still in full force.   Doubtless, the

day will come when even they will be
repealed ; but it will unquestionably not
really put the Catholics beyond the reach
of suffering. There is another persecution,
the result of bigotry and prejudice : a persecution in home life of the affections and
feelings. It sheds no blood ; it wears no
halo of martyrdom : but I can imagine it
will be very nearly as difficult to bear,
though certainly not so apparently glorious
as that endured by, for example, the ancestors of this family."

" That is possible," replied the princess,
" but even that must drop by degrees ;
and, besides, it is less likely to embrace so
large a number of sufferers. Prejudice is
like the miasma in some parts of Italy :
it covers one acre of land, and the spot
adjoining it is free from it ; and then it
shifts from place to place, creeping over
the ground like the foul unwholesome thing
it is. But a change of wind will blow it
away, and restore fresh air and healthful-
ness."

It was not many days after the above

conversation that a plan was arranged for the ladies and children, and the three gentlemen, to go to Raymond Castle, and spend the day there. The princess wished to see the castle, and Roger seemed pleased at having the opportunity of showing civility to his sister-in-law's relations. Teresa was still living at Nutley Hall, and so was her father.

Roger announced his intention of shortly taking up his abode at Raymond Castle, but at the same time he doubted the possibility of enduring his solitary life in a place so uncongenial to his tastes.

Lord Clifford talked again of taking his wife to Italy. In which case Roger said he should insist on his little Teresa being again consigned to the nuns. Teresa had not seen her own home for two years, and as before going to school she had always lived at Nutley Hall, she had no very distinct recollections of the castle. She was full of eager excitement about it, and asked endless questions of Rose and Mrs. Dorothy the evening before the day fixed for their visit there. Teresa was never so happy as when she could slip away to the room where Mrs. Dorothy sat generally surrounded with house-linen to mend, or Miss Rose's frocks to cut out and make; and taking a stool she would draw it near the window where Mrs. Dorothy worked, and commence her long list of inquiries.

It often happened that Rose and Andrea would join them, and then it was a very merry party, with a great clatter of small voices, and a curious mixture of English, French, and Italian conversation. Teresa knew but little of Italian, having nearly forgotten what she had learnt two years previous, when living with her aunt Angela; but Rose and Andrea were perfectly fluent in all three languages, and of the two, French came more naturally to Teresa than English.

Mrs. Dorothy having been a great traveller, in consequence of the vagrant habits of the family in which she lived, could understand what the children said to each

other in either tongue, though she gene-
rally confined her own observations to
English, because Miss Rose was apt to
criticise her pronunciation of French, and
Andrea to go into fits of laughter over her
Italian.

On this occasion all the three children
were grouped round Mrs. Dorothy. Teresa
had relinquished her little stool to Rose, as
being the youngest, and was herself sitting
in a chair, looking nearly as prim and
quite as sweet and nunlike as she did on
the night of her arrival, though the ugly
livery had given place to brighter attire.

Andrea opened the conversation by re-
minding Rose that she had promised to beg
Dorothy to tell them the exact truth about
some wonderful and supernatural appearance connected with Raymond Castle. But
Dorothy shook her head, and replied,

" I cannot talk to little children about
such things. I shall have Miss Rose
crying in the night, and Miss Teresa will
be afraid to go and live in her father's
house."

" Oh, but, Dorothy, I do know all about it, only I want to hear it again. The coachman told Andy the other day when Andy was riding, and when he came home he told me. I am not frightened, and I want to know more. You are not frightened, are you, dear Teresa ?"

" No," said Teresa, " I am not afraid of these things, and I am quite sure it will not make me afraid to live with papa. Poor papa ! he always looks so grave, I should like to live with him, and make him laugh."

" I hardly think you would do that, Miss Teresa," said Dorothy, "for you are the gravest little lady I ever saw myself. I should like to see *you* laugh a little more."

" Well then, Mrs. Dorothy, tell me about Bucklyn and Shaig, and then I will laugh."

" Now, then," said Rose, clapping her hands, " begin like a good Dolly."

" There is not much to tell, my dear children," said Dorothy, looking, nevertheless, grave and important. " It is only an idle story, I dare say, of the common people about here.

" You know, Miss Rose, the bend in the road as you go up to the castle from the Blackdean Road. When you have passed the park lodge a little way you come to some groups of trees, rather close together. It is not an avenue now, but it looks as if it had been some time or other, only several of the trees are missing, and there is a pond close to the side of the road, with a round island in it.

" Well, the story goes that long ago there was a very wicked Lord Clifford, who lived at Raymond Castle, for in those days the castle and the hall both belonged to the same person.

" This wicked Lord Clifford had murdered his wife, and buried her somewhere in the castle. He led a bad life, and drank hard, and oppressed the poor. One day a holy Franciscan came to Lord Clifford to ask an alms. The baron was going out hunting. He wore a broad hunting-belt, with a great gold buckle, and he had very fierce dogs,

for he was going to hunt the wolf in the
great forest under the hill. The friar
asked for alms for his house, and for the
poor of the neighbouring hamlet, and he
upbraided Lord Clifford for his cruelty to
the widow and the orphan. He was a bold
man that barefooted friar, but he said what
he said for love of God and Our Lady. The
wicked baron got very angry, and swore at
the friar, and, as the friar would not be
silent, he struck him with his great hunt-
ing-whip on the mouth, and the blood
flowed. Then he called to his savage dogs,
and they flew at the friar. They grew mad
at the sight of blood, and they tore the friar
down on the ground, and there he lay half
dead. But as Lord Clifford was riding off
the friar called out, 'Lord Clifford, Lord
Clifford, I forgive thee; but the Evil One
will ride with thee to-night, and hold by
the buckle of thy belt.'

" Lord Clifford called off his hounds, and
they followed the hunt through all the day;
but when evening came Lord Clifford was
missing. The huntsmen and the guests

heard screams far off in the forest, but he never came back. Only all through the night they heard the sound of a horse galloping, as if backwards and forwards, just along that piece of the road opposite the small pond with the island. The horse never reached the castle, but went up and down the same distance along the road, as if the rider never could find his way home. And they do say that sometimes the labourers, returning home at night, have seen a horse at full gallop : there sits on him a man pale and horrid, and holding on behind, with his arms round his waist, is the devil, for all the world like a very shaggy wolf, and the peasants call it the Bucklyn Shaig ; and I have been told that occasionally when some persons who perhaps had not a very clear conscience (for I cannot believe it would happen to a good man), have been riding down that part of the road, Bucklyn Shaig who seems always to haunt the place, will jump up behind the unhappy man and throw his arms round hi waist, as he is seen to do round the phantom

Lord Clifford, and so will ride with him, whether he will or no, till he passes out of the shade of the trees again into the open road and over the brook; and then the devil leaps down and jumps over the fence in the shape of a black cat.* And the story goes, that when Bucklyn Shaig is seen it is always a sign that some great crime has been committed up at the castle, or that a great misfortune is about to happen to the house of Clifford."

There was a pause of hushed terror when Dorothy came to the end of her story. It was too near home not to take double effect on the little listeners. Teresa's white cheek was curdled with horror, and Rosa's eyes were open to their widest stretch. Andrea was the first person to speak. He put his arm round Rosa's neck, and said:

" Never mind, Rosy, dear; if ever you and I, and Teresa see him, we will say the

* The same legend, under the same name, exists also in the county of Surrey, near Reigate. But in that case the devil disappears in the form of a shaggy dog. after crossing the brook with the rider.

Litany, and that is sure to send the devil away."

Mrs. Dorothy, seeing that her story had even more telling effect than she had anticipated, said cheerfully :

" There now, you silly children, you all look as scared as if you had seen it yourselves. Let us think of something else. Suppose we sing the Litany, all four of us together, to that pretty tune I was teaching you last week. I wonder if you have forgotten it."

Teresa's voice was remarkably sweet. She sang with much feeling, and Mrs. Dorothy, as she looked at the pure oval of her face, and the full, thickly-fringed lids, half-closing over the dark eyes, remembered some of the pictures of St. Cecilia that she had seen in her travels. She could not take her eyes off the earnest, lovely face, and when the singing was over, and cheerfulness restored, she said to herself, " That child looks as if she would die a saint one of these days."

CHAPTER IV.

A DAY'S PLEASURE.

THE weather proving favourable for the expedition—not a very long one—to Raymond Castle, the children were packed in a char-à-banc, Madame de Bray and Mrs. Dorothy being in attendance. The ladies and gentlemen proceeded in an open carriage.

When they approached that part of the park near Raymond Castle which answered to Mrs. Dorothy's description of the haunt of the Bucklyn Shaig, Andrea drew nearer to Rose and whispered to her :

" This is the place, Rose; but he will not come now, because it is daylight. I hope we shall return after dark, and so see him."

" No," said Rose, very gravely, " it is not right to wish to see such things. I cannot think how any one can wish to see the devil; and, besides, it always means, when it is seen, that some misfortune is to happen to the Cliffords; and you know, Andy, it might mean that I was to die, and you would not like that."

Rose spoke with all the confidence of a person well aware of her own importance, and particularly of the importance she must necessarily have in the eyes of Andrea. Rose remarked the little circular pond, and the island planted with willows and osiers, making, probably, a cover for the nests of some of the wildfowl that frequented the waters of Raymond Park. She noticed it then, and ever after; and many years later, when that tiny island became a most important spot to her on a dark night, the events of which we shall have to relate, Rose, in spite of her terror then, and her danger, remembered that bright summer's morning, and the drive in the char-à-banc, and little Andrea sitting by her side.

They drove past the great Scotch firs, leaving them to the left. Angela remarked that they faintly reminded her of the stone pines of her own land, and were at all events not a bad substitute ; and presently they alighted under the open, arched porch of the great clock-tower.

Teresa kept very much to the society of Mrs. Dorothy. She had found that the nurse had known her mother before her own birth, which had cost that mother's life. Dorothy was a native of the place, and had been in the family from her earliest girlhood. Teresa would ask many questions about her mother, and, above all, had begged Dorothy to be sure and get the key of her mother's oratory, that she might visit again the spot consecrated by her mother's prayers.

The entrance of Raymond Castle led into a long gallery, which ran from one end of the castle to the other, and was hung on either side with family portraits. From the centre of this gallery rose the great oak staircase, dividing halfway up into two flights of steps, and with a large window of painted glass at the top of the first flight. At the extreme end of the gallery, to the right, was the banqueting-hall, with richly-carved roof, and beautiful faces looking down from the ends of the beams. Opposite the door of the banqueting-hall was a small reception-room with a deep oriel window, and beyond that a tiny boudoir; then came Mr. Clifford's study. The larger reception-rooms were the opposite side of the gallery. The whole had been modernized from the time when the wicked lord lived there, and when the Bucklyn and Shaig was a well-recognised inhabitant of the neighbour-hood. There were, moreover, no bare-footed friars to come to the door and beg for the poor of Christ.

The old castle had been modernized in every way, and, doubtless, was less uncom-fortable than in the ages of faith, when it was also more picturesque. It retained, however, enough of its old character for Rose some years hence, as we shall find, still to call it gloomy.

Wyverns and griffins, and creatures that were neither dog nor cat, were carved outside on the posterns of the doors and mullions of the windows; the great tower, especially on the outside, was a perfect menagerie of stone monsters, who seemed ready to pounce upon you as you passed in or out of the porch through the open arches.

The children ran about in all directions, and were pleased and amused with everything. The deer came up to the very windows of the castle, and the peacocks— of which there were many, because the late Mrs. Clifford had liked to see them majestically walking backwards and forwards on the lawn—perched in the large trees near the castle, like turkeys in a farmyard.

When Teresa had accompanied the two other children for some time in their wanderings, she slipped quietly away to look for Mrs. Dorothy, and ask for the key to her mother's oratory. Mrs. Dorothy was soon found, and they went together. As we have said before, it had always been Mrs. Dorothy's care to keep it as it had been left by Mrs. Clifford. And as Mrs. Dorothy seemed to belong equally to both branches of the family, residing with Miss Rose when Miss Teresa was in the convent, and following the latter to the castle when her father took her there, she had no difficulty in getting access to the oratory whenever her pious self-imposed duties called her there.

Teresa passed into the little room with a feeling of awe. It was connected in her mind with a love she had never known, that of a mother, and with all that was most sacred in religion. The two were blended in her young mind in a beautiful and mysterious way—the past, in the thought of her saintly mother ; the present, in the thought of her own orphaned condition; and the future, in the dear hope of joining that mother in a world the reality and the nearness of which were the strongest feelings in her innocent mind.

In contrast with all the rest of the castle, the oratory, its altar, and all the decora-

tions, were purely Roman. Over the altar
hung a beautiful Ecce Homo, by Guer-
cino. The mournful dark eyes in that
pallid Face seemed to look down upon you
pleadingly. The hair, streaked with the
dews of agony, fell in disorder across the
brow; the flesh tints showed the livid
tinge that suffering gives when it stagnates
the blood. The meek Hands, so often
raised to heal and to bless, were knotted
together with a coarse cord, and the cruel
pressure had left the fingers numb and
reddened. A dark crimson drapery fell
from the shoulders as low as the waist, and
threw up in greater relief the pallor of the
figure. The coldest could not have looked
on that picture without feeling its beauty.
And the effect was heightened by the
oratory being dimly lighted by two windows high up, and shaded by blinds of a
deep gold-colour. There stood on the
super-altar an ivory crucifix, said to have
been carved by Benvenuto Cellini, and
four massive silver candlesticks. There
were no flowers. The altar itself was of

white marble, inlaid with Alexandrian mosaic. Above was a baldacchino of crimson velvet edged and fringed with gold. The walls were painted with arabesques like those of the loggie in the Vatican, and three feet from the ground ran a border of deep Etruscan red. The floor was inlaid with different coloured woods. It might have been a cardinal's private oratory caught up from Rome, and dropped in the midst of a gothic English castle.

There was something very striking in the contrast to the young imagination of Teresa. Her mother had died in Italy—lay buried in Italy. Her brief life had known, as was evident by the decorations she had chosen for her oratory, a strange sympathy with the art and artistic feeling of that land; and it was there she had gone to die, as if it were the her land of predilection, and that she would better rest in its bosom.

In after years Teresa spent many hours in this little oratory, and the thought of a mother's love, never really known on earth to her, grew into her mind with her mother's religion, and helped her to penetrate some of its deepest mysteries. As Teresa knelt on the altar steps, she prayed for that father, her only living parent, who never knelt there himself, and cared so little for the spot that should have been rendered doubly sacred by the memory of his young and devoted wife.

They suffer who dwell on the memory of the dead. But those are more to be pitied who have not heart enough to cherish the thoughts of the once beloved ones who are gone before.

While Teresa was still kneeling there, Angela and the princess came in. They, too, knelt. Presently Teresa rose to leave the oratory; Angela looked up and saw that the dear child's cheeks were wet with tears. She caught her in her arms, and pressed her passionately to her bosom.

"My child, my darling child! you have a Mother in heaven."

"Oh, that She may pray for my poor father on earth!" was the unexpected and solemn answer of that premature heart.

Already Teresa had entered upon her vocation—to live for others, and not for herself, to see the wants of others more than her own, and if it might be, even to die for others.

When Teresa left the oratory, she joined the other children, and was at once a child again. When her father came in she ran up to him and slipped her little hand in his, and seemed to watch him and keep close to him all through the remainder of the day. He turned his dark eyes upon her from time to time with a look of anxiety, if not of tenderness. He seemed puzzled at the little creature's ways, and did not know how to meet them.

Angela, with a woman's instinct, was understanding it all, and quickly perceiving how at that moment she might possibly achieve her own benevolent ends, she quietly made up to Roger, and laying her hand gently on his arm, said :

" You will let me keep her, will you

not, Roger? The poor child is mother-less!"

Roger for a moment looked troubled, a flush passed over his pallid cheeks, but he replied:

" Thank you, my dear kind sister-in-law. When you next go to Italy, I should be glad she went with you as far as Paris. If you go this winter let it be then. Meanwhile, as you are so good as to wish it, I will leave her with you, at least for another month or two."

Angela expressed her thanks warmly, small as the concession amounted to, and would have done so still more had she not perceived that it seemed painful to Roger to dwell on the subject. The old jealousy of the elder brother, and the greater house, was still gnawing at his heart, and he was too proud to give it up even at Angela's entreaties, or for any love that he might bear to Teresa. Angela tried to put in a word for Robert, now eighteen years of age, and always away from his family and his father's house. But she saw that it was worse than useless to do so, and therefore gave up the attempt, thankful at least to have carried the day so far as Teresa was concerned. And in triumph she hastened to acquaint the princess with her success.

The gentlemen had been walking all through the grounds and over the castle. Lord Clifford had been warmly praising the improvements made by his brother. And the prince had been comparing the older parts of the castle with his own feudal castle of Bracciano, where there is still to be seen an awful keep, down which prisoners were thrown in the good old times. It was quite in the body of the castle, and bears some resemblance to an enormous well. The prince asked Roger if he remembered it.

" Oh, yes," said Roger, "and I too have something of the kind, somewhere or other in my castle, only it is of a much more harmless nature. It is in fact an old well which happens to be built over, but which *does* lie underneath the flooring of some one of the rooms."

When the prince and Roger were both
in the decline of life, the former heard
something which recalled to his recollection
this trifling remark about the well. But
we must not anticipate events.

The sun had set, and the moon was
shining bright when they left the castle.
They returned home by another way—not
going through the lodge at the end of the
road, said to be frequented by the Bucklyn
Shaig, but passing out of the park into the
fields of the home-farm, and thus regaining
the road at the head of the lake. This was
done in consequence of a hint given to Lady
Clifford by Mrs. Dorothy, who was not
without fear that the children, already in an
excited state, might allow their imagination to master their judgment on the question of spectres and goblins, if they returned
home through the fatal avenue. They were
pleased with the change of road, and failed
to discover the reason, and were moreover
too merry, and too full of wild spirits for
the recollection of the Bucklyn Shaig to
have any influence

Several weeks had passed in this quiet way, the members of the one family satisfied with each other's society, but still from time time showing due hospitality to their neighbours. No one talked of going yet, and even Roger seemed contented. It is true, slight causes of disapprobation were occasionally detected by the prince and princess, and still more so by Angela, with regard to a certain tone in Roger's conversation. But Lord Clifford could perceive nothing but the brilliancy of a clever man of the world. He referred to his brother in everything, took his advice in all matters of business, and seemed to desire nothing so much as to make him feel that he associated him in every interest of his life. He talked a great deal about Robert, and the deep interest he felt in the lad, now eighteen years of age. But at the same time he said nothing sufficient to make the Orsinis perceive more in his affection than what was natural from an uncle to an only nephew, especially as having no son of his own, although he might still hope for one, the probability was that the title would ultimately devolve upon Robert. The property he had entirely in his own power, and of course would leave it all to Rose, on whom he perfectly doted.

At length, however, this unbroken calm was destined to be slightly disturbed; and, as generally happens, the disturbance came from the less prominent actors in the domestic scene.

One morning early, while Angela was sitting writing letters in her boudoir, Mrs. Dorothy knocked at the door, and begged to speak to her ladyship. Upon obtaining admission she closed the door carefully behind her, and began in rather a low voice, as though still afraid she might be overheard:

"I beg your pardon, my lady, for coming to trouble you. Your ladyship knows I never like to bring tales of the other servants, or to repeat unnecessarily anything that goes on amongst them; and I should be the more anxious not to do so in the present case, because I seem to belong, as

it were, to Mr. Clifford as well as to you
and my lord, seeing that I am nurse to
Miss Teresa, as well as to Miss Rose, whenever the former is in England. But I
think, my lady, in the present case I should
be doing wrong if I did not speak out respecting the way things are going on down-
stairs, and which, but for me, your ladyship
might perhaps never hear of till something
dreadful happened."

"Yes, Dorothy, what is it?"

"Why, my lady, Mr. Vincenzo, with his
foreign ways, has brought about quite a
change in this peaceful and christian house,
as any way it used to be before he set his
foot within the doors and darkened them.
I do not mean to say that the servants
would not sometimes of an evening, when
work was done, have a quiet game of cards,
like Patience, or Beggar-my-neighbour, and
such like, and may be they would have
penny or halfpenny stakes. But that was
the very utmost of the gambling I ever saw
in this house till Mr. Vincenzo came. But
now, my lady, it is shilling points every

night, and even half-crowns sometimes.
And this has been going on some time, till
last night they got to playing with dice
into the bargain, Vincenzo and his lordship's valet, James. It seems that James
was fool enough to be telling all the world
that his aunt as died last year had left him
a very pretty sum of money, and ever since
that fellow, Vincenzo, has been enticing the
poor fellow to play with him. And James
has played every night this week. And he
had the bad luck to win, my lady. For I
call it bad luck, since it was that made the
poor fool go on with it. Well, my lady, last
night they both sat down to it again, as if
they were in right good earnest. My opinion
is, that James was not quite what he should
have been. It was after supper, you know,
my lady, and I think as how James had
had a drop more than was good for him.
And Mr. Vincenzo, he saw that, and if he
had been an honest man he would not have
played with a poor fellow who was just a
little muddled. Well, my lady, they sat up
till three o'clock in the morning, and that

poor silly James he lost all, or nearly all. And he was like to go mad. And somehow he got spirits in, and when he found how he had lost and lost, he began drinking. The other servants, when they got up at six o'clock this morning, they found him lying on the floor of the servants' hall, mad drunk, and tearing his hair, and saying as Mr. Vincenzo had ruined him. Well, my lady, they persuaded him to go quietly to bed at last, and there he is now, and my lord was told, when Richard carried up his hot water, that James was not very well. They say he does go on so, and he says he is ruined, and shall blow his brains out. I thought it but right your ladyship should know how matters are going on. And neither the housekeeper nor the butler like to speak for fear of bringing poor James into more trouble, and he is so troubled already. But, for my part, I lay the blame on Mr. Vincenzo. He is a regular sharper, my lady, that's what he is; and the sooner he is gone the better for all the servants in this house. There is not one of them but believes the cards had been tampered with."

Lady Clifford listened horror-struck. This was the man Roger kept about him, and had done so for years. Could he be ignorant of what a scoundrel he was? At any rate she was determined such things should not continue in her house, and resolved to speak to Lord Clifford, and beg him to get his brother to prohibit his servant tempting the others to gamble while stopping at Nutley Hall; while he, on his part, would give out that the next time he heard of anything of the kind taking place, all the parties concerned should be dismissed.

Lord Clifford looked very grave about it, for he had very conscientious views with regard to his duty towards his dependants. Both he and Angela agreed that it would be cruel to punish James any further by dismissal, as he had already suffered so much. But Lord Clifford took the first opportunity of speaking to his brother about it. Roger seemed very greatly annoyed, and assured him nothing of the kind should happen again. To Lord Clifford his manner remained as before this incident, and he was always charming in his conduct to him. Of course it was the same with regard to the prince and princess, who could have nothing to do with this domestic disturbance. But he became more reserved to Angela. If possible he was even more attentive than before, but there was an absence of all affection in his manner. He was scrupulously polite, and positively waited on her wants; but he seldom talked to her, and when he did it was somewhat coldly, and as if he were only performing a necessary act of courtesy to the lady of the house and his brother's wife.

Angela felt it acutely, and complained of it to the princess. The latter perceived it, but made light of it, being anxious that her friend's sensitive nature should not dwell upon it.

Shortly after this event, which had slightly troubled the whole party with the exception of Lord Clifford—who, the thing once over, did not seem to perceive the results—Roger left Nutley Hall. He remained at the castle for about a week, and then suddenly reappeared one morning early, to say he was come to wish them farewell, as he was going that night to London, and to Paris in a few days. He took leave of Teresa with more show of feeling than he had yet evinced to his little daughter, and he finally arranged that she should remain with Lord and Lady Clifford until they went to Italy, whenever that might be; and that when they went they should leave her at the convent in Paris on their way.

Angela had greatly recovered her health in the course of the summer, and when the Orsinis left England in the beginning of October, she was hoping to be able to remain at Nutley through the winter; for, as she said, it enabled her to keep Teresa with her for some time longer, and also it was better for Rose, at her tender age, to remain quietly at home. Rose spent a whole day in tears when Andrea departed; and he, with protestations of inviolable fidelity, assured her when next he came to England it would be to make her his wife, and take her away with him. But before that period could arrive, Rose herself was to visit Italy.

CHAPTER V.

THE PRODIGAL AT HOME.

THE time was come when the Orsinis were to return to Italy, and Angela, whose restored health had induced her to relinquish the intention of leaving home that winter, was looking forward with dread to the hour of parting. It was settled they should all go together to London, and that the Orsinis should take leave of the Cliffords there.

A long day's journey, in two heavy family coaches, lay before them; but to them it appeared neither tedious nor uninteresting. The princess, on the contrary, was in admiration at the rapidity with which the English coachman and horses conducted them. They stopped at a pretty way-side inn to dine and sleep, and the shades of evening, on the following day, had closed in before they reached Wimbledon Common; and climbing up the steep hill that led to it from Kingston-on-Thames, arrived at the most precarious part of their journey, that locality being specially infested with highwaymen.

The whole party had from time to time left the carriage, and refreshed their cramped limbs by walking up some of the hills; but on reaching the too notorious common in question, it was considered too dark to do otherwise than get over the ground quickly, and hasten towards the safety of the suburbs.

Andrea had been inquiring if there were likely to be any banditti on the road, and was not altogether displeased to find that even Englishmen, who seemed to him to be for ever boasting of their superiority, lived (in those days) in a wholesome fear of highwaymen. Only when he ascertained that there were no mountains, into the recesses of which the victims were carried, and from thence were either ransomed by their friends or, failing that, hung on the nearest tree, he looked upon Dick Turpin and his class as very inferior to the more desperate and more thoroughly organised bands that sometimes descend upon poor travellers from the heights above Terracina, and despoil them of all.

A wood lay to their left, with wooden palings and with handsome park gates, surmounted by griffins; on the other hand, a yellow sand-bank, covered with golden furze-bushes; and here the road was so steep that the horses had to walk; but not even the coachman alighted. Urging on his tired steeds, he was anxious to be safe beyond the wild heath that lay before him.

Soon they were in the broad, dimly-lighted main street of Fulham, innocent of gas; and now crossing Putney Bridge, over the silver Thames, flowing silently in the moonlight, and with the square tower of the old church reflected in a broken image on the eddies rippling in the night-wind.

And now they reach the great metropolis, and, passing through the turnpike at Hyde Park Corner, alighted weary and hungry at the mansion of the Clifford's in Piccadilly.

Those were the days when Foote and Garrick acted, when Oliver Goldsmith dressed in a canary-coloured coat, and the ponderous Johnson perversely Latinized the English language, and so bequeathed it to us. But we have nothing to do with all that. Ours is a story of life as it might have been in almost any modern time, and we are anxious not to alienate our readers from sympathy with the characters in our book, by proving to them that our heroes and heroines lived differently and spoke differently from what we do ourselves in our own times. Trifling as these things may seem, our habits of thought are too much mixed up with them for us not to be strongly influenced by them. We find a deeper interest, perhaps, in the great and heroic deeds of those whose names have been consecrated by time and history. But stories of domestic life must be cast in our own mould for us to care about them. We therefore leave our friends to visit the sights and attend the theatres of a very different London from ours ; and the Orsinis having quitted its fogs for their own bright Florence, we follow Lord and Lady Clifford back to the deep shades of Nutley Hall.

The winter set in early, and the quiet routine of her home life presented few stirring events to kindle the warm imagination of Angela's Italian nature. But she possessed to the fullest measure the quiet intensity that belongs to the Roman character. Not excitable, like the Neapolitans; not treacherous, like the Piedmontese; calm, grand, and patient, unless violently roused — then for one moment will the passive depths of those Roman souls boil up in an overwhelming outburst. The deep passion that lurks in those black eyes, and hovers round those chiselled lips, takes their owner by storm. Deeds, that an instant before they could not contemplate, are in a moment executed, almost as much

to the surprise of the actor as of the spec-
tators. Ah! the lazy strength that lies in
those arched brows and moulds the brain of
those classic heads. Gentle as a woman,
proud as a lion, sleeping in the dreamy
sunshine of a whole Italian life, but from
time to time suddenly roused, and then
betraying intensity and power, intellect and
emotion, unknown to our northern lands.
Beware of the quiet patience that seems so
all-enduring; beware of a submission that
is akin to indolence and indifference. One
word may change the modern Roman so
suddenly and so completely that if you ever,
under his stolid idleness, doubted that the
blood of the old heroes was still mingling
in his veins, you would be surprised and
startled at the contrast between the lion
sleeping and the lion roused. And yet the
noble instincts of the past have died out of
them, if the hotter passions have not. Dis-
trustful in their friendships (we doubt if a
Roman trusts even his own shadow), yet
yielding a ready credulity to any charlatan
who will flatter their indolence and their

vanity; arrogant and proud, yet mean, and even sordid in private life; a people commanding the greatest variety of qualities and character under a singularly uniform exterior; the deepest of politicians and the most inane of idlers; capacity and genius almost beyond limit, or a narrow groove of uneducated stupidity; a people difficult to love (unless love can exist without trust), and yet impossible to hate!

Angela was too happy in her domestic life to pine for excitement. Wrapped up in her husband, and devoting to him the concentrated love of her nature, undivided by the affection that, had she married in her own land, she would have shared with other family ties, and constantly occupied in the care of Rose and Teresa, the time never hung heavy. Her musical talents were a greater resource to her than reading, for Italian women read but little. It could not, however, be said by any one who knew her well that her mind was uneducated. She had received that education which is derived less from books than gathered by a naturally inquiring mind from all the objects about her. She had a retentive memory, and nothing said before her escaped her notice. In addition to these qualities, she had a deep fund of poetic feeling, which threw a charm to herself over all she saw, and to others over all she said or did. Angela had never written a line of poetry in her life, but she had a rhythm in her thoughts which gave harmony to her words and her actions.

It is very rare to find any but our own countrywomen who have a true feeling for nature. You seldom see a Frenchwoman who can tell you the names of the wild flowers, if you take a walk with her through the fields, or who knows the notes of the birds in the hedges, and can give you an idea of their habits. They have not that passionate love of nature that is far from uncommon in any well-bred young English girl, and which imparts a freshness to her mind and gives a charm to her quiet country life that no Paris-bred, convent-educated French girl ever possesses. Of course there are exceptions, but they are rare ; and in good proof of it you will find that the French rarely succeed in landscape painting, and are only now beginning to appreciate the beautiful English school of watercolours.

Not all the reading that ever young lady was subjected to, not even all the variety of languages she may have studied (and few things impart more pliability to the fancy and more vitality to the power of the intellect in a woman, than a free practical knowledge of several languages), will give the charm to a woman's character in home life that she possesses by having acquired an early and a loving appreciation of external nature. The text book of Creation is a volume that spreads its own freshness and sunlight over those who study it. Perhaps it is a prejudice, but we never could feel ourselves likely to be greatly taken by any woman who had not on the whole a preference for the country. It is true, even to being trite : "God made the country and man made the town."

Angela formed one of the rare exceptions to the general rule of foreign women. She loved the country and she understood it. She did not limit her ideas of going into the country to three or four days, possibly weeks, of the hottest weather spent in an impossible dwelling called a villa, and destitute of everything that can make life practicable for any period beyond the dog-days; a house in which you start as a first principle on the fact that there never can be any serious occupation carried on within its walls, and that when the severity of the sun has a little subsided you hasten to quit and return to the capital; resuming the existence of useful mortals after a brief interval of being simply nymphs. Angela had in all this respect learnt to be a thorough English lady. She had her garden, and her conservatories, and her trim lawns. But she loved, too, the wild-brier in the hedge, and the eglantine. She knew the spots where the *Stella hostilia* bespangled the ground with its pure white blossoms, and could tell you the haunts where the

violets grew, blue and white. The tall fox-
glove, the scarlet poppy, and the fern had
a place in the china vases of her boudoir, in
company with the stephanotis and the
rarest roses. And it was in these things
that the purity of her nature betrayed itself
furtively, while it reigned and governed in
the large-hearted charity of her relations
with the poor; and in the broad, warm, un-
prejudiced sympathy she could feel with
all classes, and even with all persons, where
vice and vulgarity did not utterly obscure
the original divine work. And even where
it did, pity and not contempt covered her
words and actions.

It need hardly be said that with such a
companion Lord Clifford's married life was
a very happy one. He was proud of his
beautiful and gifted Italian wife. She
bloomed like an exotic flower in the low
woodlands of Nutley Hall. The neighbours
looked upon her as such, and might have
been envious had not her warm demonstrative cordiality taken the quiet country
people by storm, and turned emulation into

worship. She spoke English perfectly, with just enough foreign accent to account for the ring in the rich tones of her Italian voice. Her words seemed to soar above you in the air, and then fall full and vibrating on your ear like the notes of an organ. . And all the while the eyes played and glanced in their liquid depths, letting down the long fringed curtains of the lids, and raising them so suddenly as to produce a perpetual effect of light and shade in that glorious warm-tinted face. In all the events of common life she was calm and genial. The nervous fretful excitability so common amongst us Northerners was unknown and quite incomprehensible to the calm and rather slow appreciations of Angela's more stately organization. The mistake of a servant, the accidental failure of a domestic arrangement, no more ruffled her temper than the summer breath impresses the waters of the Albano Lake, lying in its fathomless depth in the heart of an extinct volcano. But when her feelings were roused, they were roused like a very storm, making her whole being quiver to its centre, and threatening to shatter her reason. But the storm passed soon, and religion had so tempered its violence that though life seemed still to quail beneath the blast, her faith stood firm and spoke of submission.

Like most characters of this class, there was a wonderful tenacity in her sorrow. It seemed to pass off, and even beneath its influence her life with her husband was no less genial and full of charm. But one who knew her well would find from time to time that the point of the dagger had broke in the wound and rankled there, sapping her life, but making no outward sign. Mrs. Clifford's death had been one of these sorrows, and her health had failed from that hour.

The long visit of the princess had done a great deal to cheer her, and consequently to benefit her health; and now the having again possession of Teresa was a constant balm to her heart. She had a passion for children, and never saw a beggar's child, with the grand look of innocence and the bold, dignified confidence the baby blends with his utter helplessness, without feeling that she longed to have it for her own, and be to it a mother.

Angela's health seemed so nearly restored that no question was mooted about leaving home again. The winter passed pleasantly, receiving their neighbours, returning their visits, and superintending the education of the two children.

It was during this winter that Robert with his father's consent, came for a short time as a guest to Nutley Hall. Lord and Lady Clifford had not seen him except very briefly on their return from Italy through Paris, for some years, and both were anxious to judge for themselves of what he was in character and appearance. They could not conceal from themselves that there was much in Robert to give them uneasiness. He had the polished manners of a French gentleman of that day, but in spite of that there was a taste for the society of his inferiors which occasioned Lord Clifford considerable annoyance. With his own family he was polished, but false. With inferiors he was loud and coarse. He was not sparkling in conversation, but he was nevertheless a good scholar, and had much of his father's versatility, but less brilliancy. He spent great part of his time up at the castle. He had brought Vincenzo with him, but the latter had orders to remain at the castle until Robert returned to Paris. Mr. Clifford said that he had some business which he wished Vincenzo to execute at the castle. Probably he did not choose that the man should stop at Nutley after the disturbance he had occasioned the preceding summer. Robert had full permission to ride his father's hunters. And Lord Clifford used to be rather annoyed by Robert from time to time declining to return to Nutley Hall, and saying he found it more convenient to sleep at the castle. He began by remonstrating with Robert on what sounded likely to be a very dull and solitary way of spending the evening, and thinking that Robert might not have ordered his groom to come and fetch back his hunter from the hall, he assured him that made no difference, and that the horse could be put up in his stables. But Robert persisted, and Lord Clifford soon found out that the evenings were not spent alone, but that Robert was joined by one or two of the least respectable of the squireens of the neighbourhood, and Lord Clifford had reason to fear that drinking formed the principal amusement up to a late hour of the night.

It was very difficult for Lord Clifford to interfere. It was the first time he had ever been allowed to have Robert with him, and he shrank from anything that would make the young man dislike his first visit to his family, which he feared any remonstrance, however kindly given, certainly would do. It was still more difficult to communicate with Mr. Clifford on the subject. It would almost have seemed like saying to him, " It has turned out as I warned you it would do, from the strange education you have given Robert."

Lord Clifford determined, therefore, to watch his opportunity, and trust to accident making an opening for him to speak quietly and calmly to Robert about his associates.

A few days after Lord Clifford had come to this determination, the hounds were to meet in Raymond Park. Robert had slept at the castle the previous night, upon some excuse or other, and Lord Clifford, therefore, did not see him till they were at the cover side. It was one of those beautiful days, in the month of February, that come to us occasionally towards the close of winter — days full of the promise of spring. There had been a protracted frost, and a heavy snow storm a few days previous. A rapid thaw had divested the earth of her white shroud, and now the sun had regained his power, the raw dampness of the thaw had passed, and a genial moist wind fanned the cheeks of the eager hunters.

The lark had begun to make mid-heaven musical. The wildfowl on the lake were sudden and clamorous in their call to each other across the water. The primroses and violets had not yet appeared ; but you were

tempted to look for them, and found yourself, in an unreasoning way, peering at the
few tufts of green leaves in the hedges, as
if you thought they, perhaps, might have
mistaken the time, and decided on coming
in flower a month too soon.

Who has not felt themselves, after the
experience of years, still childish enough to
forget, from time to time, " that one swallow
does not make a summer ?"

There was a large field that bright February morning. Angela had driven to the
meet in an open carriage, and both the
girls were on their ponies. Most of the
gentlemen were already at the cover-side
before Robert made his appearance. Lord
Clifford had once or twice asked Teresa if
she had seen her brother, and she perceived
he was getting anxious at his not arriving,
and was on the point of asking whether she
should ride to the castle, which was close
by, and find out if he were not going to
hunt that day. But before she could execute her intention Robert appeared, and
two companions with him, mounted on his

father's horses, and certainly not having much the appearance of gentlemen. They did not seem to be at all accustomed to the seat they now occupied, and they held their bridles very much as if they were squaring arms to pull at the oar. Lord Clifford pitied his brother's hunters whose mouths were subjected to such steering of the curb and snaffle. The men had each a short pipe in their mouths. One displayed a deep red muffler, and the other a bright blue one. In short, they were unmistakably more used to "riding the main" than bestriding a horse. These were Robert's companions. He himself came cantering up with them, looking so thoroughly at ease on his horse, so well, and yet not too well dressed for sport—so calm and gentleman-like, that it seemed wonderful he should find any pleasure in the society of such men. He rode to another part of the field away from his uncle, and took no other notice of Lady Clifford, and his sister and cousin, than just to lift his hat as he cantered past. Lord Clifford kept watching his nephew with more anxiety than he watched the hounds, and certainly his day's sport seemed likely to be spoiled by all he thought and felt about what he saw. In the course of the day, several gentlemen asked him who those strange-looking men were who had ridden to cover with Robert? Lord Clifford tried, in reply, to ascertain whether his interlocutors could give him any information.

"Indeed, I do not know who they are," said his lordship, " nor where Robert picked them up. One of them hardly looks like an Englishman."

"I am sure he is not," said the gentleman in reply, " I heard him swear in too good French, on the other side of that last fence you took and which he evidently did not like, to be a native anywhere this side of the Channel. But the other, I think, is English. My own impression is they are smugglers. My bailiff had to go to B——— the other day about a team of horses I knew were for sale at a farm close to the coast, and as he was going into a public-house in the town, he saw that Italian valet of Mr. Clifford's coming out of the house, and to his surprise, your nephew was close behind him. My man Harris knew Mr. Robert, and the valet knew Harris; and the Italian Vincenzo—is not that his name?—whispered something to Mr. Robert, who looked vexed, and the two walked off. Harris stepped back into the public-house and called for another glass, because he rather wanted to find out what young Mr. lifford could be doing there."

"And did he learn anything?" asked Lord Clifford.

"Well, really, I hardly like to say what he did hear, because I feel it may be making mischief; and I know what I have to say must be very disagreeable to you."

"Still I should be obliged to you to tell me all," said Lord Clifford; "I am responsible to my brother for the lad's welfare, and I have for some time been apprehensive all was not right. He is much more at the castle than at the hall. Of course, he is at liberty to stay in his own house instead of mine, if he pleases, and since his father has given him permission. But at the same time, when he is there I have no control over his actions, nor am I even sure that he always *is* at the castle when he is not at the hall. He may be out for a day or a night, and I know nothing of it, and I have no opinion of that Italian valet of my brother's."

" Well, then, Lord Clifford, I am afraid he was out for a day and a night at the very least, when my bailiff saw him. He got the landlord into conversation, and asked him if he knew the parties that had just left ? He replied, he knew Mr. Vincent very well, and that he suspected the other was young Mr. Clifford; but that he did not want to say anything. It was nothing to him who came to his house, so long as they behaved well while they were there. By degrees, Harris found out just this much —that that fellow Vincenzo is more than suspected of having dealings with the smugglers along that coast. He was often backwards and forwards there, even when Mr. Clifford was at home. And it seems that he has been down once or twice within the last month, and Mr. Robert with him. Before he left the place, he ascertained that it was said the way the smugglers had been carrying on their business lately had got to such a pass that the coast-guard was about to be strengthened. And one of these days, there will be a regular fight between the smugglers and the coast-guard, and I only hope your young nephew is not rash enough ever to take part in these excursions for the sake of the adventure, and, perhaps, get into the fray and be wounded, or taken up."

" I am very glad you have told me," said Lord Clifford; " I must see about it, and speak to the foolish lad before more harm comes of it. I wish my brother would part with that Genoese servant of his. I am afraid the man is a sad rascal."

At this moment the huntsman rang out a view-halloo, the hounds had scented a second fox, and setting spurs to their horses, Lord Clifford and his informant were dash-

ing across the plain, flying over the fence;
and out of sight and out of mind were
Robert and the smugglers, and all dangers,
however imminent, save always the danger
of losing the hounds. Everything was
forgotten for the next forty minutes. A
capital run—the best of the season. They
knew the fox well, he had given them the
slip three weeks before; but this time they
were sure of him. A fresh westerly wind
blowing in your face as you galloped over
the smooth turf of those undulating hills,
a good horse under you who is enjoying
the sport as much as yourself, and whom
you know you can perfectly trust over that
rather awkward fence with a ditch the
other side that you and he are both equally
eager to leap, the melodious notes of the
hounds in full cry, just in front of you, tails
straight, noses well to the ground—on they
go!—in at that gap—take care of the
stragglers!—over the hedge after them,
and in at the death! Not the most devoted
of uncles could be expected to be thinking
of a scapegrace of a nephew during such a

time as that! Neither did Lord Clifford. And when, slowly riding home, he recollected all he had heard, Robert was nowhere to be seen. They sat down to dinner an hour and a half after time that evening. Robert was not there. Of course, he had gone back to the castle. In the morning, Lord Clifford would see him, and with this resolve dismissed the anxious subject from his thoughts.

CHAPTER VI.

THE FISHERMAN'S HUT.

THE low coast opposite the straggling village of B—— (since then become a little town of some importance) was a well-known resort of smugglers. The country was perfectly flat for some distance inland, which deprived the coast-guard of the advantage of any eminence from whence to watch the slippery little crafts that managed to sail in and out of those deep, tide-fretted creeks so often, under shelter of a dark night.

Moreover, in those days, unhappily for the coast-guard, the sympathies of the population were far more generally enlisted in favour of French cognac, French lace,

and Lyons silks, than of His Majesty's
revenue. Malicious tongues would even go
so far as to wonder how it was that the
parson, not a very rich man, was able to
afford a few bottles of real champagne, not
made from his own gooseberry bushes, at
the dinner he gave somewhen at Christmas
tide. No one wore such beautiful gloves as
his rather pretty little wife, and somehow her
friends had reason to complain that she
never would tell where she bought them,
nor acknowledge what she paid for them.
One thing is certain, namely, that in the
obscure village of B—— and in its near
neighbourhood, you could, if you only
knew how to set about it, procure occasionally and cheaply a variety of small luxuries
not always to be 'got in the great metropolis,
unless you were able to pay a very high
price. You could not always depend upon
getting things exactly at the season you most
required them. It was all a chance, as it
were. For instance, you were far more
likely to be able to obtain a pretty light
summer silk, somewhere in the gloomy days

of November, than during the bright days and short nights of May and June. In short, like all other bargains, the occasional wares of that sea-side place were bought when you could get them a great deal more than when you wanted them.

The morning after the good run we have described in the last chapter, the westerly wind had brought on a fine drizzling rain, and it seemed thoroughly set in for a wet day. The murky clouds hung low, the breeze sighed in the barren branches, every twig hanging out a diamond drop; and under foot the decaying brown leaves were saturated with moisture, and when you stepped on them emitted a sound like treading on sponges.

Lord Clifford was still loitering over his paper and the breakfast-table, when Teresa came in and said:

"Uncle George, I have had a message from Robert to say he is gone up to London for a day or two; that he meant to have come to see you and Aunt Angela before doing so, but the morning being so wet he

thought he had better go straight to Blackdean to catch the coach."

Lord Clifford's brow clouded, and he
looked a little puzzled at this message.
After a moment's reflection, he replied :

"Why, the coach does not start for
London till one o'clock. What has made
him go so early? Who brought the
message, Teresa?"

"William, the groom, uncle ; he asked to
see me."

Lord Clifford rang the bell, and desired
the servant to send William to the door.
When he appeared, Lord Clifford said :

"At what hour did Mr. Robert leave,
William?"

"At eight o'clock, my lord."

"And where do you say he is gone?"

"I was to tell Miss Teresa, my lord, he
was gone to London."

"Who did he take with him, and what
arrangements did he make for the gig and
horse coming back from Blackdean?"

"He has taken Mr. Vincenzo ; and the
two gentlemen who were stopping there,

my lord, they have gone in their own trap that they came in, but whether or no they have gone to London, I can't say; but Mr. Robert did not give any orders about the gig. I asked Mr. Robert if I were to meet it, but he told me the horse would be safe enough. I was to mind my own business, he said, and give that message to Miss Teresa, and nothing more. That's all I know about it, my lord."

And that was evidently all anybody knew about it. It seemed more than improbable that Robert was gone to Blackdean, or to London; where then was he gone? He had Vincenzo with him, who was old enough to know what he was about; but with Lord Clifford's opinion of the man, this gave him but small assurance that his nephew was not likely to get into some scrape of a serious nature. Lord Clifford sent a groom on horseback to the inn at Blackdean to inquire. The gig had not been left there, neither were Mr. Robert's and Vincenzo's names booked at the coach-office as passengers to London by the

" Telegraph," starting that afternoon at one o'clock from the "Half Moon" inn.

It was a mystery and an anxious one. But Lord Clifford could do nothing but wait and hope for the best.

The weather was quite as gloomy, though not quite so wet, down by the sea-coast of B—— as it was at Nutley Hall on the morning we have described. The wind rose more fitfully, and moaned more sadly over those low sands and wide shingly beach than even among the trees of Raymond Park. Black masses of cloud scurried across the sky and hung low on the horizon, and towards evening there ran a long line of pale yellow light, just where sea and sky seemed to mingle in one, which spoke ominously of coming storm.

In spite of the apparent flat surface of the coast, when you came to walk along it you found that there was a succession of sand-drifts formed into banks, many of which were twenty feet high at least. In stormy weather, when the tide was high, the sea ran far up into these narrow creeks, but the action of the wind had carried on the sand beyond any point the water reached, even in the roughest weather. On the land side of these sand-banks there was a salt-marsh, broken here and there by dry patches of land, and nowhere very deep. The marshy ground was treacherous, for you fancied yourself about to walk on the greenest and most beautiful moss, when suddenly it gave way beneath your tread, and you found your footing anything but secure. Prickly sea-plants and yellow sea-thistles grew on the top of these sand-banks, not in any great profusion, but sufficient to repeat on land the pale glaucous green of the summer sea.

Leaning against one of the deepest of these sand-banks, you might have found a low, thatched cottage. As you clambered up to the top of the bank a curl of blue smoke surprised you ; for you might almost have stepped down upon the thatched roof of the humble habitation beneath you before you became aware of its presence. It stood sheltered and concealed between

two sand-drifts. The building consisted of
the ground floor, and a few low bedrooms in
the roof. It was a curious, rambling habitation. There seemed to be several out-
houses, a stable for two or three horses,
and a shed for a cart; but all so crowded
together, and so small in each compartment,
that it looked much like the fragment of an
Irish village.

At about twelve o'clock on the same day
the two nautical gentlemen, whom we have
already seen so much out of their element in
Lord Clifford's happy hunting-fields, were
to be met coasting along the marshy ground
to the inland side of the sand-ridge we have
just described. They were smoking as usual.
But they had left their trap at a friend's
house in the village, and had come about a
mile on foot. The elder of the two gave a
low and peculiar whistle, as he stood by the
closed door of the house. The windows
were rather high up in the wall, and the two
that were visible in front were not much
larger than a good-sized pocket-handker-
chief. There was no reply to the low

whistle, no sound of life from inside the cottage door. The elder man turned to the younger, who was standing behind him, and was looking up at the window as if he expected to see some token that the house was not empty.

" I say, Jacques," said the elder man, " I guess Annette will understand your whistle better than mine. You try."

Jacques blushed as deep a red as his own voluminous neck-tie, and uttered another whistle in quite another key. The effect was instantaneous. They heard the taking down of a bar and the drawing of bolts, and presently in the open doorway, stood as bright and beautiful a maiden as ever gladdened cottage or palace.

Annette Barrow, the smuggler's daughter, was about seventeen. Ned Barrow was an honest (so he thought himself) English fisherman. But as the fish that came most readily to his net swarmed nearer the French than the English coast, Ned Barrow had fallen in love, some twenty years ago, with a dark-browed, rough-voiced

Frenchwoman; so that Annette might be said to belong to either nation, and certainly had gleaned her own fair portion from the merits of each. She wore a full, short, red petticoat, her dark blue skirt was looped up over it by the skirt being pulled through the pocket-holes. The bodice was tight fitting to the neatest figure and the trimmest waist that ever were seen. The sleeves of the bodice were short, ending in a lappet a little below the shoulders; but there were tight red sleeves matching the petticoat, below the lappets. The sleeves were neatly buttoned round the wrist of a little white dimpled hand with rosy-tipped fingers, that gleamed and flitted before you, and seemed now close to you, and now snatched away from you as Annette laid the table and prepared the dinner or sat at her work, in a way that was perfectly bewildering, and which, whether you would or no, you could not help observing. A small head, crowned with rather wavy black hair, which grew low and thick upon her white brow; and thicker still, and

without a single straggling hair, round
the nape of her ivory neck; two laughing
eyes with very long under lashes; full,
round red lips, and teeth so small and even
that they resembled the dazzling pearls in
an infant's mouth; a warm smooth complexion, and a ringing voice, with a slight
foreign accent; all combined to make
Annette one of the most fascinating of
maidens, and certainly entitled her to the
place she held in the affections of the
bronzed, bearded, and handsome young man
who answered to the name of Jacques, and
who was a French ally of the English
smugglers.

Ned Barrow chucked her under the chin
as he entered the cottage, and Jacques,
under cover of his intended father-in-law's
broad shoulders, caught the little hand that
lifted the latch, and kissed it.

" Annette, child, where is madame ?" said
Ned, looking round the small room.

" She is gone father, on the rocks now
the tide is out, to pick up some small crabs
for supper."

" Gone out for crabs! You do not mean it? What does she know of where to find them ?"

" Oh!" said Annette, laughing, " I mean real crabs this time, father."

" I see, I see," said Ned. " Well, Annette, there are two gentlemen coming down here this evening, and you must get them a better supper than usual. I will provide the wine if you and madame will take care the fish is well dressed, and madame will have some of her nice little French dishes that I never can remember the names of, though I am very fond of eating them. They will be here before dusk. We expect some of our men in to-night with a good cargo, and these gentlemen are friends of ours."

Our readers will need to be told what is the difference between catching real crabs and only catching crabs allegorically.

It often happened that the smugglers returned from their excursion with only a few kegs of brandy or hollands, under cover of night when the tide was low. It was not always advisable or necessary to take the booty inland, as the risk thereby was increased, and if incurred, the means of executing it in safety must have been previously arranged and secured with those who were to receive it. Under these circumstances it was usual to excavate the sand round the base of some of the low rocks, slippery with green sea-weed, which covered the sands for at least a quarter of a mile out to sea. Of course the rocks that offered the best facility for this were known to the smugglers. Such as stood beetling over the sand afforded a slight temporary shelter; or in some cases several low small rocks would enclose a little space of sand, where a hole could easily be dug, and a keg of spirits rapidly and safely buried.

Annette knew the rocks, and understood the signs of a recent deposit, and it was her duty to carry a large basket and a small spade, and after dusk, or very early in the day, to go what was technically called, crab-catching.

It must be borne in mind, that all these

smugglers were ostensibly fishermen, and there was nothing calculated to attract attention in the fisherman's daughter being frequently down by the sea-side, nor in her carrying a large basket to help bring home some of her father's fish. Nor was it altogether without just reason, that we have mentioned the fact that Annette wore a very full red petticoat; for, independent of its being the custom amongst the fishermen's wives to have garments of this description, it not unfrequently happened that Annette's under clothing was partially composed of rolls of very valuable lace, and therefore it was convenient that her robes should be ample and well adapted to convey any slight additional bulk that might be introduced beneath the folds of her skirt.

It was not long before madame returned from her excursion, a sufficiently successful one for Annette to declare she should furnish the guests with crab soup for that night's supper.

There was a peculiar fascination in the *life*

the fishermen and smugglers led. Apart from
the grave fact that they lived on the viola-
tion of their country's laws, they were not,
on the whole, such bad men as might have
been expected from this one great moral
delinquency.

As fishermen they were a peaceful, brave-
hearted race, characterized by the frankness
and simplicity peculiar to those who live on
the wide trackless fields of ocean, and draw
their first and strongest impressions from
the simple majesty and stern grandeur of
the deep waters. They would (as a class)
have shrunk from highway robbery, or from
the mildest form of picking pockets. But to
cheat the revenue was not, in their estima-
tion, like robbing a man. The revenue
was an impersonal power with which they
had no sympathy ; an abstract principle of
a tyrannical nature from which they were
free to escape whenever they could.

It is true that Annette, though brought
up in the midst of it, had at times serious
misgivings as to its being a right mode of
life, arising chiefly from the fact that to

carry on that part of her father's business
required so much caution and deception, a
thing from which her innocent nature recoiled. Annette had been, when quite a
child, educated in France, for at the commencement of his married life, Ned Barrow
had carried on his trade of fisherman, and
his practice of smuggler, the other side of the
channel, in the little seaport village where
he had become acquainted with the bold,
dark-browed Frenchwoman, now universally called madame. There Annette had
gone to school, and learnt her catechism
under the care of the good old curé, and had
never omitted going to church on Sundays
and holidays, her father not having objected
to his daughter being brought up in her
mother's faith. She used to lament that in
England they were so far from any Catholic
chapel—there was none nearer than Nutley
—and sometimes would speak of it to her
mother. When she did so she perceived
something in madame's manner that be-
tokened an impression that there was that
in their present mode of life which was

incompatible with a strict performance of their religious duties. Annette would look puzzled and anxious, but madame would soon turn the conversation, ending by an affectionate caress, and a prophecy that her pretty Annette should some day marry, and leave the fisherman's hut, and live like a lady, and go to church when she pleased.

But Annette loved Jacques, and Jacques too was a fisherman and a smuggler, and so there seemed to the poor girl no end to the painful mystery of right and wrong, and no chance of any light breaking in upon her conscientious doubts. But Annette had not forgotten the prayers she had learned at the end of her catechism, and she said them faithfully every night, with a certain hope that some day she should know more and be better guided. Meanwhile, she obeyed her father, respected her mother, and, above all, loved Jacques.

And now the fisherman's cottage became a busy scene of preparation. Madame and Annette consulted on what they should lay before their expected guests, and the men shortly after left the house and went on their separate business. Ned Barrow was going carefully to reconnoitre the various hiding-places known to the fishermen, and to form conjectures as to the exact spot where the party of fishermen returning home that night were most likely to land.

Jacques went into the village and visited certain houses where he was well known, and communicated the intelligence of the expected return of the fishing-boats, and of the necessity for some of their people being at hand to convey the cargo on shore and carry it safely and secretly away to their various domiciles. He was then at a given hour to meet Robert Clifford and Vincenzo in a spot already decided upon by the latter, to whom this place was well known, and so bring them both unobserved to the fisherman's cottage; they having left the horse and gig at a wayside inn.

At about eight o'clock that evening the white cloth covered the large table in Madame Barrow's front kitchen, the crab soup simmered in the bain-marie (one of the many French treasures that madame had embarked with her when she came over to England, a three days' stormy voyage in her husband's fishing-smack), and the whole house was redolent with the odour of fried fish. The fisherman's lad who lived in the house with them and went errands, and mended the nets through the long summer evenings, had been sent by Annette to the village to procure some fresh bread and other articles, and had just returned, and Madame Barrow was asking what sort of a night it was, and whether he had heard any news up in the village.

Frank—for that was his name—had come in with an expression that seemed to denote he had important news to communicate, if only any one would be so good as to think it worth while to inquire of him.

" It is a dark, bad night, madame. There is a drizzling rain now; but the wind is getting up. We shall have a regular sou'-wester before midnight. I hope our fellows will be able to land before it gets too bad to attempt it. But that is not the worst, madame, that I have got to say. I stepped in for a few minutes at the 'Three Fishermen,' and I heard some men, sitting drinking in the bar-room, who were talking about some new fellows as have been sent down to join the coast-guard. Some say there are two more men, and some say four. Anyhow, one thing is certain, the force is stronger than it was, and we must keep a double sharp look-out to-night. They only came this morning; it is a pity as we had not known it sooner."

Madame's brow darkened. Annette turned pale.

" Did you see anything of the gentlemen your master is expecting here to-night, Frank," said madame.

" Well, I saw their horse and gig, for they have put it up at the 'Three Fishermen."

" I wonder what they are coming for," said madame. " We shall have quite work enough on our hands, if there is any scuffle between our men and the coast-guard, without having strangers, and landsmen too, who know nothing about it, to look after. I don't mind Mr. Vincenzo of course, because he is an old customer; but I don't trust young gentlemen who come out of their way to spend an evening in a poor fisherman's hut. It can be no good they come after, and I'll tell you what it is, Annette," said madame, looking anxiously at her daughter, and lowering her voice as Frank left the kitchen, "I won't have these land-sharks coming after my pretty daughter, and making love to her, recollect that."

" I am sure, mother, I do not want them," said Annette, turning very red and looking offended; "and you know *that* very well, mother. I do not know why you should suddenly suppose they are coming on my account. I have never seen the young gentleman, and as for Mr. Vincenzo who comes so often, you know I cannot endure him, and always get out of his way when I can."

" Well, well, child, I did not mean to hurt you, only you know I am suspicious of any one who comes here, unless it be all in the way of business; and if you find the young gentleman is in the way you can go to bed early; I'll engage your father shall not object."

It was not long before Ned Barrow returned, and madame communicated to him the tidings brought by Frank. The lad was sent for and made to repeat his story. It might be true, but it was too vague and uncertain to be relied upon. Nevertheless, it was better to be on the safe side, and Frank was sent off again, this time on horseback (for as we have already told our readers, there was stabling connected with the cottage, and Frank, though a fisherman's boy, could ride, at least as well as Ned and Jacques, whom we saw not long ago out hunting), and under cover of night, to give notice to their friends in the neighbourhood, that they might muster in good force at a certain point, and be prepared to overpower the coast-guard by numbers, if there were a surprise, and they were driven to defend themselves.

Ned Barrow was at the head of the smugglers on this part of the coast; and, as our readers have no doubt perceived, not a man in indigent circumstances. He was the chief of a clan of fishermen; he owned nearly all the skiffs employed in fishing on that coast; for in those days, when fishing and smuggling were so often combined, it had become an organized business; one requiring discretion and prudence in the leaders, and necessitating some command of men and boats.

Frank had not returned from his mission, when Jacques' low whistle was heard at the door, and on madame cautiously opening it, he came in, with Robert Clifford and Vincenzo.

Annette was placing on the table some glasses reserved for the guests, the members of the family drinking out of horn mugs. She turned her head as the men entered, and Robert thought he had seldom seen a brighter looking being. He took off his hat, and bowed to her, as he would have done to a lady in her own drawing-room. Annette bowed slightly, but took no notice of Vincenzo. The time had been when the sly Italian had tried to snatch a kiss. Annette had deeply resented it, and partly the remembrance of this, and partly the presence of his young master, made Vincenzo quietly keep in the background.

Robert was awed by Annette's great beauty and natural dignity. He talked to the fisherman's daughter as he would have done to one of his own rank; and though he scarcely took his eyes off her sweet face, there was nothing over bold in his manner. He soon perceived also how matters stood between her and Jacques, and in spite of his growing love for low company and low adventure, he was still too much of a gentleman not to behave with discretion and delicacy towards his host's daughter and his fellow-guests. He was only twenty years of age, and might still have been reclaimed from his evil courses, had any kind friend been at hand to influence him.

The night was fast closing in. Frank had returned from the village. The fishermen and smugglers were by degrees mustering in the neighbourhood of Ned Barrow's cottage. A low whistle, a pass-word, a mysterious rap at the door, and one after the other of the roughly-clad, and well-muffled clan stood in the glare of the fisherman's wood-fire and couple of oil-lamps that filled the kitchen with a red light.

There was evidently a strong impression of fear amongst the smugglers that their friends expected to land that night, and supposed to bring some valuable booty with them besides fish, would be surprised by the coast-guard. There was a vague suspicion that something was about to happen. Every one had heard that the number of the coast-guard had been increased, yet no one could tell from whence the rumour came.

According to the state of the tide, they expected the boats in about midnight. Till then, Ned Barrow's cottage was a perpetual shifting scene of men coming and going, orders given to scouts sent to watch from different points, and those returning from time to time to state that all was quiet.

Meanwhile, the dark pall of night had fallen on the blackened waters. The wind had risen wild and blustering. The rain pattered on the windows, and the blast tore round the house with a deep groan, ending in a shrill scream, and sobbing fitfully between the gusts. The stars were hidden by the dark masses of rolling cloud, and nothing could be seen on the great expanse of heaving waters, save the white-crested heads of the great breakers, riding on with tossed foam, like white-maned horses; then bursting on the beach with the booming sound of cannon, and drawing back again their shattered waters with a harsh hissing on the pebbly beach.

It was an awful night. Little children lay awake in their cots with wide open eyes, wondering if the wind were the voice of the lost souls. The fishermen's wives sat up feeding the fire and listening for footsteps; the pious and the good prayed for the poor mariners; and the happy thanked God for safety and shelter through that wild storm.

But in Ned Barrow's cottage there was riot and noise, singing and drinking, throwing dice, and eager disputes. The red glare flashed on bronzed faces and swarthy brows. There were French among the guests as well as English, and there were landsmen from the village, who were in close league with the smugglers, and carried on the contraband trade in the country.

It was a new page in rough life to Robert. Dashing and daring himself, vitiated by an evil education, but full of energy and youthful curiosity, he was delighted at, for once, realizing one of those wild nights in the smuggler's cottage, that Vincenzo had so often described to him. He came for a mere freak, but once there, he threw himself into the rough amusement of the house with all the energy of intemperate youth. Vincenzo was at home there, and through the riotous mirth had little odds and ends of business of his own to transact, and was wily enough to keep cool and sober to the last.

In the midst of the uproar, Ned Barrow never for a moment lost sight of the real cause of this gathering of his men. While doing the honours of his house to his guests, and superintending and directing all, the watchers returned from time to time from their stations on the coast, and he gave his orders calmly and distinctly. In anticipation of a possible attack, the men were to be armed, and their pistols were examined and their cutlasses sharpened, amid tales of daring adventure, loud choruses of hearty sea-songs, and toasts drunk in real good cognac.

Long before the guests had become thoroughly riotous, the two women had retired to their chambers. Madame was not, however, intending to go to rest. She came backwards and forwards as her husband called her, or as she perceived anything was wanted in the kitchen where the smugglers sat. She took no part in the revel, but she watched the orgies like a grim priestess, and ministered to the wants of the motley crew gathered beneath her low roof.

Annette was supposed to be in bed and asleep. But there was no thought of sleep in Annette's large, anxious eyes. A presentiment of evil crept over her heart, and made her restless and wakeful. She did not undress, but moved about her small room, opening and shutting drawers, arranging trifles that did not need it, and then, suddenly standing still in the middle of the room, would listen to the loud winds, or bend her ear to the noise below, and fancy she could catch the sounds of Jacques' voice, and would wish him away from such scenes, and herself too; and as the night grew on Annette became more nervous and more restless.

By degrees the sounds of riot below grew fainter, she heard the door open and shut, as one by one the smugglers went forth to meet again at various points along the coast. She opened the door again and listened. She heard the door open at the foot of the stairs, that led into the kitchen; there was a dim light in the passage. It was Jacques standing at the foot of the stairs. What did he want? She came out upon the landing. He whispered her name, and in a moment Annette was by his side.

"I wanted to wish you good-night, Annette. I am going now. It is a rough night, and something tells me our fellows will not land in safety."

There was a tone of sadness in his voice.

"Why do you go, Jacques?" she said, slipping her small hand into his brawny palm.

"Why do I go, my little one? What a question! I go to bring you a silk dress, or something else you will like as well." He said this lightly, then, drawing her nearer, added softly, "One kiss, Annette, before we part. Think of me. We shall meet again soon."

Annette granted the one kiss, and a vague dread pierced her heart as Jacques spoke. Quick as thought, she took a small

black cord that she wore round her neck,
with a crucifix attached to it, and holding
it to his lips to kiss, passed the cord over
his head, and said :

" Keep that, and think of It and me."

He hid the sacred image in his breast,
and the tears started to his eyes.

" One day, Annette, you and I will leave
all this," flinging his hand contemptuously
towards the room where the loud voices of
the revellers were heard, " and live as we
thought to have done when M. le Curé
taught us our catechism together. Pray
for that, Annette."

Before she had time to answer he had
turned suddenly away, and with one quick
parting look of affection, not unmixed with
anxiety, he closed the door behind him, and
was gone.

Annette paused. He had hardly re-entered the room when one of the others made
some jesting remark, to which Jacques
replied with a ringing laugh. In another
moment she heard him say he was ready to
go. One or two others declared their inten-

tion of accompanying him, and Annette listened to the retreating footsteps.

Sadly and slowly she crept back to her little room. Why did it look so empty, so desolate? The ceiling seemed to press down upon her brow, the four walls to close in upon her. The trim little nest where Annette had slept away so many peaceful nights seemed like a prison to her now. Her heart beat loud and fast with anxiety and vague dread. What was the heavy weight at her heart? And yet she was glad Jacques had spoken those words. He too, she thought, was weary of this rough life: he, like herself, was more than doubtful of its being right. He had reminded her of the days when he used to call at their cottage in France, to take her with him on Sunday afternoons to the catechizing in the church. They were neighbours, and as he was the eldest he was trusted to see the little Annette safe through the streets to the old parish church, and back again. Their courtship had begun in those early days, and now poor Jacques, like

Annette, was pining for the lost innocence and peacefulness of that long past, but unforgotten time. Annette knelt down by the side of her little bed. Against the wall hung the Image of the Crucified, and with many tears she prayed that redeeming mercy might take compassion on her and on him she loved, and that they might ere long make their peace with God and man, and live within the laws of both.

The night wore on, but the storm continued with unabated violence, and neither madame nor Annette went to bed, though the former looked in once or twice and remonstrated with the latter for sitting up. At length both women, feeling the need of each other's company, though neither openly avowed it, relinquished all idea of sleep, until the party should return home ; and they gave themselves deliberately up to watching the storm. Wildly it whistled round and round the house, with a spiteful capriciousness that seemed like the working of an evil spirit. The wind rose with a shrill scream, and then seemed to lie down and moan like a creature in pain. Sometimes madame opened the door a few inches and peered out into the dark night, but, seeing nothing save blackness, she would climb to one of the upper windows and try to discover a light in the distance, or to hear any sound beyond the surging of the waves and the roaring of the wind.

They kept the fire alight, and sat hovering over it. At length madame, leaning back in the gaunt, wooden arm-chair, that had been made tolerably comfortable by a collection of cushions covered with patch-work tucked into all parts of the back, arms, and seat, fell into a doze, starting from time to time in her uneasy sleep, and relapsing again against her will.

Not so Annette. With every nerve become doubly keen from anxiety, she sat and watched, and listened. Presently she began to perceive that the wind had sunk, and that the sobbing of the blast came more seldom and less loud. She ventured to open the door, and with straining eyes looked towards the sea. It was not long before she saw

dark figures, that seemed to detach themselves gradually and indistinctly from the
black air and approach towards the cottage.
She flew back, and catching her mother's
arm, awoke her with a scream. Madame
went to the door, and soon perceived two
men were carrying a third, and that behind
followed two more, one of whom seemed to
walk with difficulty.

Annette was the first to recognise the
form of the wounded man, who was carried
by Frank and one of the fishermen. She
gave a stifled cry, and madame, at the same
moment catching sight of Jacques' death-
like face, said to her :

" Go in, Annette—go in, my child."

Annette stood behind her mother, rooted
to the spot; nothing but force would have
made her go in at that moment. In another
second the five men had entered the house,
and the wounded man was laid on the
ground. He had fainted; the blood was
flowing from a sabre cut in his breast.

In a moment madame and Annette fetched
a mattress, which was laid on a large

chest, and a temporary bed made for the sufferer.

A few words told the whole story. They had been watched when and where they least apprehended it. There was a supposition that one of their own men had betrayed them. While aiding the. landing of the fishermen, whom they had that night expected, the coast-guard had suddenly come down upon them. Such of the boats as had not landed their men put back to sea. The men had drawn their cutlasses. One of the coast-guard was killed. Jacques had received a mortal wound in attempting to rescue Ned Barrow, who was taken prisoner by two of the coast-guard. Robert Clifford had received a cut on the leg, in the midst of the fray, and had been hurried away by Vincenzo, without whose aid he was unable to walk.

Several of the fishermen and smugglers that escaped came to the cottage, each with his own account of that night's disaster.

The scene that a few hours before had been óne of loud revelry was now one of anguish and horror. In the midst of her unutterable anxiety and despair about her husband, madame had to attend to the two wounded men.

Robert Clifford was impatient to depart. His wound was not serious, but the lameness it caused rendered it impossible he should return to Raymond Castle or Nutley Hall, without being exposed to inconvenient questioning and consequent discovery. After a brief council with Vincenzo, it was decided that, as the term of his intended stay in England was nearly at a close, they should go up to London with their own gig and horse, and that, when sufficiently recovered, Robert should return to Paris. He could account, by any plausible untruth, for having met with a slight accident, and would take care to be off before there could be any question of Lord Clifford's going up to see him. The coach did not go every day from Blackdean to London; and though Lord Clifford, with what was universally considered his eccentric and extraordinary habit of taking his foreign wife frequently abroad, was a most unusual exception, yet he was incapable of " running up to town " in the easy way of more modern times, even those nearer our own day, but before the invention of railroads. It was settled that Frank should ride over to Raymond, and take a note to William, the contents of which he was to communicate to no one, appointing him to meet them in London on a certain day, and bring back the gig and horse.

They had stanched the blood that flowed from Jacques' more serious wound; and madame, with streaming eyes and gestures of despair, was binding up the slight cut from which Robert Clifford was suffering; while Vincenzo had gone to the " Three Fishermen " to fetch the gig.

" Ah, sir," she said, in the midst of her sobs, " why did you ever come to the like of us ? It is not for young gentlemen like you to be frequenting poor fishermen's homes, and be getting within the grasp of those horrid men that your cruel English laws send down here for our torment.

What will become of me, now that I have lost my brave man? What will they do to him? Where will they take him? My good Ned, my poor husband!" As it was not much that could be said to her of a comforting nature, for there was little doubt of what poor Ned Barrow's fate would be, taken, as he was, red-handed, in open conflict with the representatives of those outraged rights of the revenue, her questions only led to fresh bursts of grief, and to passionate entreaties to Robert that he, being a great gentleman, would use his influence to save her husband from hanging.

Robert could make but very little reply to these entreaties, for, in point of fact, appearances were as much against him as they were against Ned Barrow, and only that he had had the good luck to escape he might have been in terror for his own neck. More than half ashamed of himself, and angry at finding himself in such a position, he betrayed no little irritation at the unhappy woman's prayers.

Vincenzo perceived the difficulty in which his master was placed, and having returned with the gig, was only extremely anxious to get him, with himself, safe out of the house.

"Now, madame," he said, pushing her away, and at the same time thrusting a piece of gold into her hand, "leave the young gentleman alone. He can do nothing for you, nor for your husband either. You are well paid with this for your night's entertainment. It is no fault of my master's, nor of mine, that Ned Barrow has got into trouble; so hold your tongue, and let us be off."

So saying, he helped the limping Robert into the gig, and prepared to follow him. He had not, however, done so before the French virago, in the heat of her rage, and the depths of her despair, had flung the golden guinea on the ground, and dealt a blow with her clenched fist at Vincenzo's face.

"Take that, you pale-faced Italian villain!" she exclaimed, with glaring eyes red with tears, and streaming weird locks hanging dishevelled over her shoulders.

"Who is it but you brings the young gentleman here to make him as bad as yourself? Don't I know your wicked practices this many a long day? Would I not be glad to see your head on top of a pike; aye, and help to put it there if I could? Beware of him, beware of him," she continued, addressing Robert, "young gentleman. You that come with a miserable valet to smoke and drink with poor fishermen. He will be the curse of your family, and the ruin of you all, if you do not heed the words of Clotilde Barrow, the fisherman's wife."

Wild with her impassioned rage, she tossed her brawny arms in the air as she spoke. Her snake-like locks, her broad bosom, her tall figure, shook and trembled as she stood, like an inspired Pythoness, on the steps of her own door, with the red glare of the fire-light behind her; while Robert and Vincenzo hurried away as the grey morn was breaking in the eastern sky.

A sweet, sad picture of a gentler sorrow than her own met the frenzied woman's eyes as she turned to enter the cottage. Annette was kneeling by the couch on which lay the ghastly form of poor Jacques. She stood still a moment, as if struck dumb with the vastness and variety of her sorrow, and gazed upon the group before her.

"You will see him, Jacques?" said Annette in a low, pleading voice. "You will let him come and help you make your peace with God? Oh, Jacques, we have deserved this, and we are punished as we deserve."

"Not you, my innocent child," he said. "You only did what you were taught, and I, who loved you, Annette, knew how pure you were, and ought to have warned you against myself, and against all around you. But what could I do, Annette? They were your own parents, and I was as bad as any. But it is all over, Annette, and the lessons of my boyhood come back upon me now, and the faith I hope to die in. So make haste, Annette, and let the priest be sent for. I have not many hours to live."

As these words fell from his lips upon the ear of Clotilde Barrow, she bent her head upon her hands, and sobbed like a child.

The priest was sent for. Frank was to call at the chapel-house on his way to Raymond Castle, and tell Father Netherby of the dying man who needed his presence, and implore him to come quickly.

At noon that day a far different scene from that midnight revel and its ghastly ending presented itself in the fisherman's cottage. The Prince of Peace Himself had been there, and the messenger of peace had spoken the last words of absolution. Still bending over the now placid face of the dying smuggler, Father Netherby was repeating to him the sweet sacred names that the Catholic tries to articulate with his last breath. Annette has ceased to weep as she kneels by the couch, gently holding the poor fingers that else had wandered clutchingly over the blood-stained sheet.

Madame Barrow, subdued and silent, stands with clasped hands at the feet of the dying man. She is the first to see that all is over, and bending her powerful arm round Annette's waist, she raises her gently, but firmly, from the ground, and draws her away with the same silly words of tender endearment with which she had striven in the years that were gone to soothe her darling in any of the sorrows of childhood. And Father Netherby drew the sheet over the dead face of the repentant sinner.

The shattered bark of his young life had been drawn into port, wrecked and broken; but its precious freight of a living soul was landed on the shores of eternity, amidst the tears of repentance and the beacon light of Faith.

CHAPTER VII.

AWAY TO THE SOUTH.

THE LADY CLIFFORD TO THE PRINCESS ORSINI.

"Nutley Hall, September 18th.

"MY DEAREST LOUISE,

"You will be grieved to hear that my fears about my own poor health, expressed in my former letter, were but too justly founded. I caught a fresh cold the beginning of this month, and the old cough and all the former symptoms have returned. And, alas! with the old malady has come back the longing to breathe again my native air—the pining for *home*; not the home of my affection, which, God knows, is here, in the land of my adoption, but the home of my girlhood, the land of my birth. I love England, with its wayward, uncertain charms and journalière beauty, the sweet surprises of its rare and unexpected warm days, and the fitful glory of its varied skies; but the moment that cold, clammy hand seizes me, that raw, damp feeling of approaching winter, back to my heart rushes all my Italian blood, and I feel, yes, dear Louise, I really feel as if I should die if I remained away from my own clear skies and transparent atmosphere. I grieve that it should be so, for I am ashamed to have married an Englishman and to be for ever dragging him away from his noble house and his home duties. I am ashamed to expose him, as it does do, to the astonishment of all his acquaintance at these wild, erratic habits, and to the weary long journey, with its perils, its risks, and enormous expense.

"The only thing that comforts me is, that George really does not dislike the long days that we sit in the family coach, behind the rough horses and the hugely-booted postilions, up hill, down dale, through tedious France.

" Even the sea passage, so dreaded by me, and so terrible in its uncertainties, has charms for him. The blood of the old sea kings runs in his veins, and has tinged his hair as it has that of my own fair Rose. I wonder we have courage to take so young a child such a fearful journey; but it would require more to leave her behind.

" I long fought against going away, and fully meant this time to have resisted George's persuasions, even at the cost of my life; but while I was doing so, and thinking I should gain my point, the more alarming symptoms were renewed. I broke a blood-vessel again, on the 10th of last month, and after that George would listen to no more arguments. My doom was sealed. Can I say I regretted it? My heart bounded with hope as, kept to my bed, silent, and fed only on ice and milk for ten days, I left all the labour of preparation to my poor husband and my friends, and lay dreaming of Rome and Italy.

"I am glad to say that Roger, who is again at the castle, intends remaining all the time of our absence. This will be of use to George, who, as you know, places unbounded confidence in his brother, and will leave much of the business of the estate in his hands. I wish Roger had allowed us to take Teresa with us to Italy. But as he will not do so, the next best thing is that she should return to the Ursuline Convent in Paris. I dread parting with the darling child more than I can express; but (you know my feelings on this point, Louise) anything is better than her having to live alone with her father at Raymond Castle. I do not think he is to be trusted with the care of a delicate and sensitive girl; and I do not believe the fact that Robert is to return next year would make it better for Teresa. Considering all the anxiety that boy has caused us, and his mysterious conduct in leaving home, and taking leave of no one, I do not imagine

he would be a good companion for Teresa.
When Roger returned a month ago he did
not seem much affected by what George
told him about Robert; and that wretched
Vincenzo is still in his service. It is a
hopeless case."

"Paris, Sept. 30.

"Ah! Louise, I write with a heavy heart.
I have parted with my sweet Teresa, that
dear child of my adoption whom I love as
my very own, and for whose welfare I feel
almost more responsible. It is doubly hard
to lose sight of the beloved child at an age
when her companionship had become so precious to me, and when every day I trace more
of her mother's mind and character, and see
in her the image of my early friend unfolding before me, and claiming a double portion
of the affection I gave to her whom I lost.

"This morning I took her to the convent
of the Ursuline nuns in the Rue d'Enfer.
You know they are strictly cloistered in that
convent, though not so in many other houses
of the same order.

" The carriage did not enter at the *porte cocher*, that privilege being allowed to royalty alone. We slipped through the little door cut in the huge gates, and Rose, Madame de Bray, myself, Teresa, and poor weeping Dorothy, stood inside a covered court, the portress's lodge on the right, a little parlour, with glass doors, on the left, and in front another pair of huge gates, barred, bolted, and chained. Beyond that is the cloistered garden. We were shown into the little glass parlour, and there waited while the portress went to announce our arrival.

" Teresa is greatly beloved in the convent, and all the community had requested to come down into the garden to receive her, as also a few of the scholars who were the child's favourite companions. Teresa had a consolation under the pain of parting that was wanting to us : she is much attached to the nuns, and felt, she said, that she was returning to a second home.

" Presently we were summoned by the portress and two externe sisters, and we stood in front of the great gates while they unbarred them, so as to throw open one half. We heard the voices of the sisters on the other side calling Teresa's name gently and softly, though by no means in whispers; and when the gate opened there stood the greater number of the good nuns waiting to welcome again their dear child. They stretched out their hands to receive her, and help her across the wooden bar, which did not open with the gate but kept us still separate from them. Teresa flung her arms round my neck, and Rose clung to her. Then in a moment, breaking from us, she skipped lightly over the bar. The reverend mother caught her in her arms, the others gathered round. The dear child looked back ; she was pale, and the tears stood in her eyes ; but she gave us a sweet smile, and kissed her hand to us. The great gate swung to, and I heard the clanking chain and the rusty bolt shutting me out from my darling, and as I turned away and wept, I felt as if it were for ever in this life.

" It was however, decided we were to

take leave of her from behind the grille in the parlour up-stairs, and accordingly we entered a long narrow room, divided by the iron grating and the black curtain down its entire length. The curtain opened, and there was again the sweet face of Teresa, with the tears all gone, and looking placid and at home. But we had had our last embrace, as no more than the tips of her little fingers could find their way through the bars, to satisfy poor little Rose's affection. I cannot get that touching picture out of my mind. Teresa clinging to the venerable mother, in her dark serge dress and black veil, and looking back upon us, her long beautiful hair having escaped from the blue ribbon that bound it, and hanging in rippling, gold-tipped ringlets round her delicate throat and her white dress. It was the image of Innocence in the arms of Religion ; and it haunts me still, sadly yet sweetly."

CHAPTER VIII.

AN OLD FRIEND.

WE must leave Lord and Lady Clifford to the happy effects of their sojourn in Rome, and Teresa to her studies in the convent, and look back upon Roger and Raymond Castle.

Judging from the immediate change in his mode of life, it appeared as if the absence of the family from Nutley Hall were a great relief to Roger. A vast deal of his moodiness seemed to pass away, the neighbours were invited to the castle; there were sounds of life and merriment going on in the usually silent halls and corridors.

Every morning Roger might be seen going out shooting with his friends. Lord

Clifford had begged that he would shoot the Nutley covers during his absence, and this of course gave Roger an opportunity of showing more sport to his neighbours than his own small estate could afford. And even this slight increase of dignity and importance was acceptable to his vanity and ambition.

Of an evening he would sit down to cards with his friends; but partly because they would have proved unwilling, and partly from a fear of scandalizing the neighbourhood and driving his companions from his society, Roger was compelled to play moderately, and for much lower stakes than was his usual habit.

It was the second autumn since the Cliffords had gone to Italy, and there was yet no talk of their return. Roger seemed to have taken to country sports, the management of his own estate, and the supervision of his brother's. It is true, from time to time a feverish restlessness would seize him and drive him to the capital for a short time to look up his old friends, visit his old haunts, and sometimes return with a party of quite a different caste from the country sporting gentlemen in the neighbourhood of Raymond Castle.

Once he went over to Paris for two months, and on his return showed, by the purchase of a couple of fine hunters, and by some improvements in the furniture of the old castle, that his visit had been a lucky one. On his return he seemed gayer than usual, and his house was still full of guests, when one bright morning in the middle of September he received the following letter from an old friend and frequent companion of his, already once alluded to in these pages, Mr. Henry Bethune. They had been acquainted as children, then had lost sight of each other, but had kept up unbroken intercourse for the last five years.

Henry Bethune, like Roger, had lived a great deal abroad, but chiefly in Germany; whereas Roger's haunts had been Paris and Florence. Nevertheless it was at Paris that they met again, in one of those *salons* not unfrequently found at the time of our story, where under the auspices of an agreeable and fascinating mistress, every luxury and the charm of agreeable society were combined with unlimited gambling. It was in one of those *salons*, of less than the *demi-monde*, that the two friends renewed their friendship. By that time both were known for desperate players. But Henry Bethune was the superior of Roger. He had a cooler head, and if possible a less scrupulous heart. It was his profession, and he excelled in it.

The blood rushed to Roger's brow as he read his friend's letter, and rapidly thought that the moment approached when once again, in such congenial companionship, he should give loose to his favourite, nay, his only passion.

The letter ran thus:

" DEAR ROGER,

" Business has called me to London for a few days, and I cannot cross that horrid channel without giving myself the pleasure

of seeing you in your own castle. Will you
receive me on Tuesday next for four nights?
We will shoot every morning (for I am told
you are devoted to sport, and are the best
shot in the county), and amuse ourselves on
the *tapis vert* every night; and you shall
give me my revenge of the money you got
out of me the last time we met at the
charming Madame Charles's. Write by return, and I will set off that day."

Roger wrote and accepted his friend's
proposal. He felt that in doing so it was
no light accidental question of seeing an old
friend again. They met to gamble and to
play deep. It might bring Roger all he
wanted, for he knew Henry Bethune was
enormously rich, or the scale might turn
against him and it would be his ruin.

The guests then in the house were all to
leave the next day in the afternoon. He
would have a clear day before him, as
Bethune could not arrive till Tuesday
night.

That evening, when Roger was preparing
for sleep, and Vincenzo was busy attending

upon his master, Roger told the man that Mr. Henry Bethune was expected the following day, and that a room must be got in readiness.

"Which room will your eccellenza prefer for Mr. Bethune?" said Vincenzo.

"Oh, it little matters which room you give him. They have all lately been inhabited; so damp as this old house is, it cannot make much difference."

There was something in Vincenzo's countenance which seemed to imply he was not altogether of his master's opinion. He hesitated a moment, and then said:

"I think, if it pleases your eccellenza, he had better sleep in the white wainscoted room."

"To be sure—to be sure. I don't care."

"Nice room that," said Vincenzo, as if aside to himself; "convenient room—just the place for Mr. Bethune. I will see it is prepared."

Roger was too well used to his Italian servant's somewhat amusing familiarity to take any notice of it in this instance.

Vincenzo passed for being eccentric as well as foreign. It rather amused Roger than otherwise, and seemed some relief to him from his own taciturn ways. Vincenzo was very useful and very devoted. Roger used sometimes jokingly to say he was his *âme damnée*, and that he believed there was nothing the man would not do to serve his master.

The next night Bethune arrived, and the two friends sat talking over past events, and inquiring about mutual friends.

" The charming Madame Charles had come to grief. Her proceedings in her gilded *salons* were too outrageous. Two degenerate gamblers had drawn knives, or daggers, or pistols, or some such thing at each other. There had been bloodshed. The police had interfered. Poor Madame Charles had retired to the provinces after a brief residence at Clichy, from whence her devoted admirers had redeemed her. But it was not thought she was likely to appear in Paris again, or at least not for some time. She was a great loss, however, to her own circle;

she had managed things so cleverly till this terrible *esclandre* took place. Perhaps, added Bethune, " she may change her name down in the provinces, and re-appear with all the past blotted out, and start afresh."

" But I thought," said Roger, " there was a Mons. Charles. Was not that respectable gentleman who used to ring for more champagne, and seemed always to know how the play stood with everybody, her husband ?"

" My dear Roger, no! that was only ' mon oncle ;' no impediment whatever to Madame Charles disposing of her fair hand elsewhere. They said there was a *tendresse* between her and the poor fool who was murdered in her drawing-room. But I dare say this was only a little bit of Parisian melodrama got up to heighten the occasion. There was a great talk about it at the time. I wonder you did not hear of it."

After more conversation in the same strain, fully betraying the tastes and habits of the two friends, they parted for the night. It was late in the following day before they met again, near noon. Roger took Bethune round his place. In the afternoon they lazily killed a few pheasants. In the evening they played. Roger won, and won much.

That night when he came to bed he was in excited spirits. Vincenzo cast one searching glance on his master's face as he entered his dressing-room, and seemed satisfied. He talked to his master about various small household affairs, and inquired what orders there were for the gamekeeper the following morning.

"Would his eccellenza go out shooting at all?"

"Oh yes, Vincenzo; for though there is better game to be had at home, yet a good walk in the open air keeps the head cool and the hand steady."

"Eccellenza has had good luck to-night?" asked the man.

"Not bad, Vincenzo, not bad. Not to be compared to that night in Florence, when I came home half drunk with wine and good fortune, and flung you mille francs as I entered the house. By Jove! I must have been drunk indeed. But I would do it again, Vincenzo, if I ever had such another run of luck as that."

"Eccellenza is very good," said the oily man. "And Mr. Bethune, how are his spirits, sir?"

"Oh, he does not mind—not much, at least. You know he is rolling in money, and by this time he has learnt to take the fickle goddess just as she is—now smiling, now frowning. His life is spent in nothing else."

"Then Mr. Bethune may sleep sound to-night," said Vincenzo, dropping his voice as if speaking to himself, "in the white wainscoted chamber."

"Why, Vincenzo?" said Roger gaily, "you seem to me to have wonderfully picked up your English. When you first came you could hardly make yourself understood. Now you can talk as fast as I can. I do believe you have been taking lessons of that pretty housemaid I caught you philandering with in the backyard the other day. Recollect, you rascal, I will not have anything of that sort going on in my model house."

" Eccellenza need not fear. I have got my English by reading. I have found your English Bible,* and have been reading that. Wonderful stories, to be sure !" (Vincenzo, as a Catholic and an Italian, had hitherto been more versed in the New than the Old Testament.) "I dare say people learn a great deal by reading them, if they can only understand them."

" Well, Vincenzo, and what did you find there ?"

" Oh, eccellenza ! I found a story about Jael, ' mother in Israel.' " She brought him butter in a lordly dish." Clever woman that,—only a chisel would be better than a nail. Very clever woman that."

Roger laughed out. " What is the man talking about ? So that is where you get your English, is it ? Well, it is a relief to know you have gone to no other source. I should have thought pretty Nancy would

* English version.

have been a more eloquent teacher than a
"mother in Israel." But you have made a
wise choice, Vincenzo. Go on and prosper.
And now put out the lights, and let me
sleep."

Vincenzo did as he was told, and closed
the door. As he did so a sinister smile
curled his thin lips as he muttered, " Per
Bacco che bestia !" (By Bacchus, what a
fool.)

The next day the same course of events
was followed. Sport in the morning, play
at night, and again Roger was successful.
When the two friends parted there was not
a shade of displeasure on Bethune's face.
Calm, serious and passionless, he had watched
thousands flow away from his possession
into that of his friend, and he had written
I O U's without a frown on his brow.
But the next morning he came down with
a more fixed expression of countenance,
and when Roger proposed they should take
their guns, he objected.

" You must give me my revenge to-day,
Roger ; and as you know I have to be off

before daybreak, I shall not sit up so late as you made me do last night. And so if you will have the table set, we will begin our play earlier to-day. By the by, have you been so good as to give orders about my going ?"

" Yes ; it is all settled. You say you know of a ship that sails for the coast of France to-morrow, and that you have taken a berth. How did you manage it? Did you see the captain, or write to him ?"

" I did neither. I sent my servant, who, as I told you, I had to dismiss for mis-conduct the very day before I came here, which is the reason I have to trouble your factotum Vincenzo, with a letter and full instructions. The skipper will not sail until I come, if, that is, I arrive at all within the mark. You tell me that part of the Sussex coast where I know the ship sails from, close to S—— is not more than twenty miles from here. Vincenzo is to drive me there, and see me on board. Was not that what you were so good as to say?"

" Oh, yes ! it is all settled ; and as you

go at such an unearthly hour, I have desired Vincenzo to see to getting the trap ready himself, and not call up the stable men. What hour will you be called?"

"Punctually at four, and I shall be off at half-past. And now, Roger, let us settle a few of the scores between you and me. It is too bad your having all the luck on your side."

The two friends sat down to their game at an earlier hour that day, and each played as if for the dear life. At first Roger's luck continued, but, after a while, whether he got over-flushed with success, or whether it was only the turn of chance, the cards were against him. Silent and unbroken the fatal game went on. Vincenzo alone was allowed to enter the room. He crept in and out noiselessly to see if anything were wanted, and each time he did so, he stole a glance at his master's face. What he saw there was explanation sufficient as to how matters were going.

It had been arranged that they should dine at an hour earlier than usual that evening.   And a good two hours before the time, Roger, with troubled brow, declared he would play no longer then.

He was pacing with hurried strides beneath the great north wall of the castle, when Vincenzo, who had seen him from one of the windows of his master's room, came to tell him that it was later than he thought, and not far from the dinner hour. Roger returned to the house and entered his own room.   To his surprise, Vincenzo, who had gone up the backstairs, came in at the same moment, and shutting the door behind him, stood silently looking at his master.

" What is the matter, Vincenzo ?   What do you want ?"

" Eccellenza," replied Vincenzo.

" Well, what is it ?"

" Something must be done, Eccellenza, Mr. Bethune must not ruin my signor. This ought to be stopped."

" How can I stop it, you fool ?   I tell you I *am* ruined.   We shall have to leave England as soon as this rascal is out of the house, unless I get back my luck this very night, and filch him of all he has robbed me of."

" And your excellence," said the servant, in his eagerness translating literally his Italian term of respect, " will let Mr. Bethune leave this house with all those little bits of paper safe in his waistcoat-pocket ?"

" Why, what can I do ? I cannot rob the man, still less can I murder him."

" Of course not, your excellence; your high-born hands must not smell of blood. Not that there need be much blood either. That Jael was a clever woman."

Roger started to his feet, white as ashes, the perspiration standing in beads upon his forehead and upper lip.

" What do you mean, man ? Speak out."

" Vincenzo slipped quickly to his master's side, and whispered in his ear:

" He sleeps in the white - wainscoted room."

" Are you mad, Vincenzo ?" roared out Roger. " What has the man's sleeping in that room to do with my losing my money?"

"Pazienza, signor, pazienza! and listen to your faithful servant. Do you forget there is a closet in that white wainscot, so well disguised that I doubt if any one in the house knows of it, but yourself and I; and I have the key."

Roger paused and reflected awhile. He remembered, in fact, that the room was wainscoted in carved panelling cut off at each corner of the room from wall to wall. It was not easy to know whether the masonry behind was in like manner squared at the corners and so lay flat with the wainscot. Probably this was not quite the case with any of them, for the wood gave a hollow sound if you rapped it. But a quick ear would have detected that one sounded more hollow than the others, and close observation would have discovered that there the panelling was not quite so closely and neatly joined. Moreover, in one of the folds of the carving, so aptly called the linen pattern because it resembles drapery, there was a small circular hole, which might possibly be the keyhole of some peculiarly-shaped lock.

Roger saw it all now. There was a closet in that angle of the room. Some one might be concealed there while Bethune slept. And then——!

It was some moments before Roger could speak. He looked as if he were about to faint. Vincenzo, calm and noiseless as a cat, walked up to his master's dressing-table, and pouring from a silver-mounted flask on the table some powerful liquor, filled up a large wineglass. Roger snatched the glass, drained it, and catching his breath twice before he could speak, said in a hoarse whisper—

" But, have you thought of all, Vincenzo—the body—how shall we hide it ? Good God ! what am I talking about ?"

" Be calm, sir, and leave it all to me. I *have* thought of all. Remember, you may get back your luck to-night. When you see which way the game is going, and are about to separate for the night, you will ring the bell for supper. If, when I bring in the tray, I see you have accidentally dropped your handkerchief close to the bell-pull, as you get up to ring, I shall know that Mr. Bethune's pocket is stuffed with those bits of paper that he must be made to give up. You will delay him long enough over the supper to give me time to conceal myself in the closet. Your excellence will wait here and leave all to me. When it is over, I will bring you Mr. Bethune's pocket-book. He will not want it again." And as he said those words, a horrid smile crossed Vincenzo's dark sallow face.

Roger listened with an expression of un-utterable horror and agony, and then, in a tone of almost irritation, hoarsely whis-pered—

" But the body, Vincenzo; you forget the body ! We shall be discovered through that."

" Tut, tut ! Vincenzo has thought of all. Does your eccellenza remember long ago my once asking you, whether it were true that this part of the house is newer than

the rest of the castle, and that in your
study down-stairs, where lately you have
always dined with Mr. Bethune, there is
under the flooring the mouth of an old
well ?”

“ Yes, it is quite true. I remember seeing it myself some six years ago, when
finding the dry-rot was in the boarding,
I had a new floor put down.”

“ We must take up the floor wherever
you tell me the well is, and now you see
how we can dispose of *the body*.”

“ The taking up of a few of the boards
will not require much time; but there are
the joists, how will you get through them,
so as to step in yourself and lift a cumbrous
weight down to the mouth of the well ?”

. “ Your excellence has ordered dinner
earlier, and it was to get to speak with you
in private that I pretended it was later
than it is. You must dine to-night in
the room in which you and Mr. Bethune
play, and though it is not likely he would
think much about that, yet, lest it should
lead to remarks after, I will light a fire now

in your study, and leaving the bag of straw in the chimney,* fill the room with smoke. You can allege the smoke as reason for not dining there. The servants will smell the smoke, and so believe you. You, meanwhile, will say you have locked both the outer cloth doors, so that no one may go accidentally into the room, and let the smoke over the house. I have got all my tools ready, and shall shut myself in there, for of course it is I and not you who really lock the doors. I begin my work as soon as you and Mr. Bethune are at dinner; the double doors will keep out the noise of my sawing through the joists and wrenching up the boards quite as well as they will the smoke. But first of all, eccellenza, you must please to go down with me, and show me exactly where the well is."

When Vincenzo had ceased speaking, Roger sat as if almost stupefied. He seemed, indeed, to have heard all, but hardly

* There were no register grates in those days, and the old fashion prevailed of stopping up the chimney as described above.

to be able to grasp the thought of cold-blooded murder, that had been so clearly and calmly laid before him. Suddenly his brow contracted, and, starting from the chair into which he had sunk, he staggered to the door.

Vincenzo followed, and in another moment they were both in Roger's study. Not far from the wall, opposite the window, and which, like the other walls of the room, was covered with well-filled book-shelves, there stood a very massive writing-desk. It had drawers on either side at the front, and a space behind for large folios, such as maps or engravings.

"There, Vincenzo; the well is just beneath that desk. We shall find it not easy to move."

In a moment, Vincenzo had taken out the heavy books behind, which added greatly to its weight, and disposing of them without leaving any trace of disorder, moved the desk, and lifted up the thick turkey carpet which covered the floor. Roger remembered the exact spot, because at the time he had already alluded to, he had cut with a penknife a small cross in the floor above the centre of the well. He had done this with no definite purpose, but simply as a reminder of where the old well had been, and had never from that day till now recollected it. The sight of that scratch seemed suddenly to bring before him some scene of the past. He remembered that Angela had come into the room at the time, and that she held Teresa by the hand. Teresa had asked what Roger was doing, and in jest he had replied, " making a black hole to put Teresa in when she is naughty." He remembered kissing the child at the same moment, to prevent the threat being an alarming one. Angela had laughed and told him he should not say such things, even in jest, to a child.

It all came before him, like a forgotten dream. Roger had always been ambitious, fond of money and irreligious; but now, he was worse than this—a murderer in intention, and soon to be one in deed.

A mist of tears, the last honest ones he will shed for a long time, came over his eyes. But at that moment the dressing bell rang out, and Vincenzo reminded him that no time must be lost.

After a few more recommendations, Vincenzo lighted a match, and set fire to the fuel already laid in the stove. In a moment, the smoke was pouring out. Roger locked the outer doors, one from inside, the other outside, and gave Vincenzo the key. Enough smoke had escaped for them to be corroborated in their statement : and having so far proceeded in their horrid scheme, Roger returned to his room to prepare for dinner, talking the while in whispers with the subtle Italian.

When Bethune came down to dinner he naturally went straight to the study door. Roger came out upon the landing before his room at the same moment; and hearing Bethune making for the study, called out to him :

"Not that room, Henry. Thinking it was a little chilly this evening, I ordered

them to light the fire, and it smokes so
confoundedly, I have been obliged to lock
it up, and desire dinner to be laid where we
were playing this morning, in the circular
room.

At the same instant Vincenzo was approaching the other door of the study from
the side near the servants' offices.   He
appeared to be carrying down a basket of
old newspapers, which his master was in
the habit of having filed.   At the bottom
of that basket lay his carpenter's tools,
concealed by the papers.   So that while
Bethune was trying one door Vincenzo
was entering the other, carrying the in-
struments for preparing the wretched man's
grave, while the blood was yet coursing
lightly in his veins, and he thinking only
of life and success.

CHAPTER IX.

WHAT THEY DID WITH HIM.

DURING the whole of dinner Bethune talked on in high spirits. His manner to Roger Clifford was easy and intimate, and somehow brought vaguely back to Roger's mind the recollection of their early days, when the two young men had really been attached to each other before the world and their love of play had darkened their hearts. Henry Bethune had been very handsome in early youth, and was so still, in spite of the rather flashy appearance which had increased of late years. Roger looked at him as he sat after dinner with his elbow on the table, and his white hand glittering with rings lightly passed through his brown hair. There were the same clear grey eyes, that would seem almost to emit sparks of fire when their owner was excited, but that were deep and tender as a woman's when no strong passions stirred his soul. And there was (and it was this which specially struck Roger at that moment), the alabaster white of the brow and temple, just where generally the brown hair fell over them, but which was now pushed aside by his hand. Roger's eyes fixed upon the white spot. Bethune looked so young! there was the delicate grain of white china in that temple. And as he looked, the words came to his mind, "but a chisel would be better than a nail." He fell back in his chair and gasped, and his hand shook as he poured himself out another glass of Madeira. The grey eyes darkened for a moment as the thought crossed Bethune, "this man is unnerved, and is drinking too much to keep a steady hand at cards to night." He got up from the table, and flinging down the napkin, exclaimed,

" Come, Roger; you are getting low
and nervous. Take your revenge of me
like a man, and if fortune does not smile
on you this time, follow me to Paris, and
you shall have it out of me there. Fair
play is fair play, you know, my lad; but I
do not want to ruin you."

Was it all fair play Bethune meant to
try that night? Roger flushed up to the
brow at his friend's words, and rang for
the table to be cleared. In another hour
the expression of both men was changed
and fixed. Roger's dark eyes were haggard
and sunk, Henry's grey eyes were cold,
keen, and hard as steel. Roger was losing.
Presently he rose from the gaming-table to
write another of those fatal papers which
were transferring Roger's and Robert's and
Teresa's fortune into the hands of Henry
Bethune.

As Roger rose to ring the bell, Bethune
asked, " At what hour, Roger, does your
post go out ?"

" Not till half-past nine. The boy rides
over with the bag to Blackdean, and sleeps

there that night, returning the following morning with the letters."

"I must write a letter to Paris," said Bethune; "do not let the bag go till I have done so."

"Bring coffee," said Roger, aloud, "and do not let the boy go with the bag till Mr. Bethune's letter is ready. You must come in again, when I ring, to fetch the letter."

While Bethune was still writing, the coffee came in, and Vincenzo put it down on the table opposite to Roger. Bethune sat at another table with his back to Roger. Presently he sprang up, just as Roger, who had asked him if he would take coffee, and been replied to in the affirmative was putting in the sugar and cream. Bethune's brow darkened. Roger was very pale, and his hand shook. Bethune mistook his action; he took the cup of coffee, and returned to the table where he had left his letter. He continued writing, folded the letter, sealed it with his signet-ring, and meanwhile said to Roger:

"Who locks your letter-bag?"

“Either I or Vincenzo. Why do you ask?”

“Because I am very particular about my letters. This one is of importance. If you do not mind, I should like to see it safe in the bag myself, and the bag locked by you in my presence. I suppose you have not two keys, have you, and that Vincenzo carries the other?”

“Here is the only key of my letter-bag, Henry,” said Roger, showing one that hung to his watch-chain, “I keep it myself, though I sometimes give it to Vincenzo to use. What are you afraid of?”

He then pulled the bell violently. Vincenzo appeared so quickly that he could not have been far from the door.

“Send the boy here with the letter-bag,” said Roger, in an irritable tone, and Vincenzo disappeared.

Presently the boy came in, much astonished at being sent for. Roger took the key, and holding open the bag for Bethune, the latter slipped in his letter. The bag was locked, and the boy went off with it.

"How particular you are," said Roger, with a sneer.

"My good fellow, there's no harm in being cautious about one's letters. None of my friends know where I am, and it is just as well they should, in case I don't get safe across that cursed channel."

"There is not a breath of wind, anyhow," said Roger, with some hesitation, for he did not half like Bethune's remark. "Have you told them the name of the ship you sail in, and the port she sails for?"

"By heavens! No. I forgot that. However, it is as well as it is. I doubt her being a very respectable craft. Indeed I happen to know she is not so. And there would be no use in my name getting perhaps mixed up with some smuggling transactions on a large scale."

It was a relief to Roger to know Bethune had not given this clue to his movements; and if he could have recalled the bag and stopped that letter, he would have done so. But it was too late.

Roger noticed that Bethune did not drink his cup of coffee, and remarked it to him.

" No," he replied, " I am afraid of it's keeping me awake, and as I have a long, cold, morning's drive before me, I am anxious to get an hour or so of sleep. Now, Roger, one more try. It is impossible that I should break off now; you must get back some of what you have lost. The chances are all in your favour. Another throw, man !"

Roger sat down doggedly, and the play was resumed; but Roger was far too nervous to be a match for his cool and wily adversary.

" I tell you what it is, Bethune," he said, starting to his feet, with an oath, " I will stand no more of this; I am a ruined man already, and, by Jove! there is not another squeeze to be got out of me."

Bethune felt that one word on his side would lead to a regular quarrel. Roger was livid, and shook from head to foot. Bethune coolly got up and said,

" As you will, my good fellow. You know where to find me in Paris, whenever you feel inclined to set yourself right again by another try at your luck."

He quietly gathered up the papers that the wretched man had signed, and clasped them in his pocket-book, which he then transferred to his waistcoat-pocket. Roger watched him, and drawing out his handkerchief, passed it across his brow: he got up to ring the bell, and in doing so, dropped his handkerchief close to the bell-pull.

Vincenzo appeared. His eyes glanced at the handkerchief on the floor, he stooped forward to pick it up, and laid it on the table near his master. Their eyes met. Vincenzo pushed the handkerchief towards him in such a way as to make him feel, as his hand lay close to it on the table, that he had slipped a key within its folds. It was the key of Roger's study-door. All therefore was ready in that direction. Roger turned very pale, but Vincenzo saw that his purpose was the same, and left the room to fetch supper. When he returned with the tray Roger began pouring out some brandy and water, and urged Bethune to have some also.

"Thank you, my good fellow," said Bethune, rather coldly. "I do not feel inclined just now; but if Vincenzo will be so good as to put a couple of fresh eggs in my room and a bottle of champagne, I shall be glad enough of them, I dare say, before I start to-morrow."

" What a strange breakfast, Henry. No, no ; Vincenzo will see you have some hot coffee."

" Nothing but the eggs and champagne, Roger. You know I have my fancies about food, and this is one of them."

Roger gave a glance to Vincenzo, as much as to say " See it done." Vincenzo understood Bethune's motive, if Roger failed to divine it, and as it did not in any way interfere with his plans, he was willing enough to supply the champagne and eggs.

About a quarter of an hour from this

time, the two friends had shaken hands in apparent good feeling, and with promises of soon meeting again. Bethune repaired to his bedroom, and the wretched Roger sought his study door. The whole household had retired to rest long ago, but, nevertheless, the sound of the key turning in the lock made Roger start. He held a candle in his hand, but as he opened the door a blast of cold air caught the flame and blew it out. Happily the fire was still alight, and the smoke dispersed, being now allowed to follow its natural course up the chimney, and by the flickering flame Roger beheld, yawning at his feet, a great black hole, from which had sprung the blast of wind. The carpet was turned up, and the boards and pieces of the joists, and the tools, lay piled up on the side of the hole. Down below, all was dark. Roger relighted his candle, and then found that Vincenzo had put his arm-chair close to the fire, and a small table by the side, with two wax, candles and a tray on which stood bottles of wine and brandy. He was to sit at his ease in luxury and warmth while his friend was being murdered above. Horrible thought! and, oh! horrible, diabolical wickedness of the cold-blooded, clever wretch who had so elaborately and so accurately planned it.

The clock struck one. The pendulum ticked loud. The gas in the coals seemed to roar. A piece of wax curled off and dropped from the candle. Every sound was agony. Roger sat, with his elbows on his knees and his chin leaning on his hands, and listened—listened.

When Henry Bethune reached his room, he found the two eggs and bottle of champagne ready for him. Having lighted the candles and taken a knife from his dressing-case, he examined the cork of the narrow, long-necked flask before him.

"Yes," he said, aloud to himself, "that cork has been pressed in by strong machinery; it has not been tampered with since, so I may safely cut the wire and drink it. And those eggs are as the good fowl laid them. She may have put a little chalk in, but no arsenic. It is a comfort there is some food prepared by nature which even one's dearest friends cannot turn into poison. I mistrust me I should not feel as well as I do had I drank Roger's coffee down-stairs."

He broke and swallowed the yolk of the two eggs, and drank off a tumbler of champagne, and he carefully locked the door and examined the windows. The height from the ground was considerable, but the shutters had not been shut. He closed them, and drew the iron bars across. He proceeded to load a brace of pocket-pistols, and put them on half-cock. He laid them on a chair by the side of the sofa, and then threw on his large travelling-cloak; he packed up his valise and dressing-case, felt that the precious pocket-book was safe in the inner pocket of his waistcoat, changed his dress-coat and boots, and laid a large neckerchief ready to tie on when called in the morning. He wound up his watch, calculated that he had rather more than two hours to sleep, tossed off the remainder of the champagne, blew out the light, and then, without a prayer or a thought, the wretched man flung himself on the sofa and was soon in deep sleep.

Little did he suspect that through one tiny hole, no bigger than a pea, every movement, so far as the range of vision through that small aperture permitted, was watched by the eye of his intended murderer. He had locked and barred himself in with the man who was waiting for his life, and now he slept in utter security.

A gleam of bright moonlight found its way through the shutters and fell across the figure and the crown of the head of the sleeping man. And there was the alabaster temple, that had arrested the gaze of Roger, again uncovered by the treacherous brown locks that fell aside from it.

The white panel of the wainscot opened, and with unshod feet the noiseless Vincenzo stepped into the moonbeams. He held in his hand a hammer and a chisel. The latter was unusually fine and sharp. " A chisel would be better than a nail," had been his running commentary on the history of Jael and Sisera. The hammer seemed out of proportion large as compared with the thin, delicate chisel; but it was not so for Vincenzo's purpose.

He crept up to the side of the sleeping man. No more light was needed than that which the cold unconscious moon bestowed. He raised the hammer suddenly, and with enormous force brought it down on the fore part of the sleeper's head, full amid the clustering brown hair. There was a groan, no more; but Vincenzo knew that his victim, though stunned, was not dead. There was a slight indenture in the centre of that white temple. A blue vein marked it like the brow of an innocent child. He held the chisel against the fair skin, just a little aslant, and avoiding the exact spot of the blue vein (for had he not said there need not be much blood?), he drove the fatal edge just into that part of the skull where the join is marked by a jagged line, and in infancy is not yet closed. It was a

skilful hand that drove in the fatal wedge.
There was not another groan. A few drops
of blood crept down the ghastly cheek, but
hardly tinged the travelling-cloak, which
Bethune had flung over the pillow and
gathered round his recumbent form.

Vincenzo stood and watched. His breath
came hissing with excitement. For a moment it deceived him; he did not know it
was only his own; but collecting himself
still more, he thrust his hand into the
wretched man's bosom. It was warm, nay,
hot with life; but there was no pulse. He
dragged forth the gold-clasped pocket-book,
and then he lighted a candle, took a look-
ing-glass, held it to his victim's face, to be
sure the surface remained unclouded, felt
his pulse, was sure, beyond all question
sure, and, blowing out the candle, groped
his way to the door. He unlocked it,
and locked it again from the outside. He
had first carefully locked the fatal closet
in the wainscot, and now, with shoeless
feet, he crept to the door of his master's
study.

Roger started up, and the two men, the murderer in will and the murderer in deed, stood face to face. But neither spoke. Vincenzo held out the gold-clasped pocket-book—the hand that held it was bloody. Roger recoiled, and Vincenzo, quietly placing it on the table, gave a slight bow, and said :

" E fatto, eccellenza " (It is done, your excellence).

Roger seized the book, now that, like a child, he was no longer scared by the sight of blood. He tore out the fatal leaves that had signed his ruin, and flung them into the greedy flames. Then both men drank the wine before them ere either seemed ready to speak or act.

" And now, Vincenzo, my friend," stammered at last the wretched Roger, " the corpse. We must dispose of it quickly. You will have to be off soon. Drive for your life to the spot on the coast that—that *he* told you of, and explain to the captain that his passenger has relinquished his intention of crossing, and has gone back to

London; but not wishing to disappoint them, as they had promised to wait for him, he sends them the fare agreed upon."

"And something over, eccellenza, to make more sure of their not grumbling, you know," added Vincenzo.

"Yes, and something over. We must get rid of all the—*his* effects—that in the morning nothing may appear beyond the fact that he is gone, as he intended, and that you are gone with him, as arranged, and are to return as soon as the mare is sufficiently rested, and that the ship has sailed; and now let us go up-stairs and bring—this thing down——"

The servants all slept at quite another part of the castle, down a long passage, cut off from this end of the building by a door. Vincenzo, to make doubly sure of no sleep-walker accidentally coming that way, had taken the additional precaution of locking that door. He had always been in the habit of sleeping in a room adjoining his master's, and therefore it might be said, that, with the exception of the room where lay the murdered man, they had the whole house to themselves.

Vincenzo lighted a candle and led the way. He unlocked the door, and the two stepped in. Roger gave one look, and turned away sick.

" Cover up the head, Vincenzo; it is too horrible !"

And yet it was not horrible—awful, but not horrible. The marble features had in death resumed the beauty they had lost under the impressions of a bad and dissolute life. The lids were closed over those once deep-grey eyes, and the long lashes, so much darker than the brown hair, lay on the colourless cheek. The clustering curls were slightly disordered, and one red, narrow line, streaked down the side of the face, alone betrayed it was death, and not sleep.

" It were better first to remove his luggage, and leave the body to the last thing," said Vincenzo. " If you will carry these into your study," pointing to the valise and dressing-case, " I will wrap up the corpse that your excellency does not like to look at, and then, between us, we can get that down afterwards."

Roger took up the candle, and passively obeyed the order of the fiend who commanded him; Vincenzo, meanwhile, drew the cloak round the corpse, congratulating himself all the time that, owing to the wretched man's having entirely covered the pillow with it, not one drop of blood had fallen on any part of the furniture.

"How lucky," said he to himself, "that he did not get into bed, and lie in the white sheets!"

It was hardly done before Roger returned. Vincenzo pointed to the feet of the dark, inanimate form that lay between them, for Roger to take up, and himself lifted the shoulders. He had confined the cloak round the body with the wretched man's own shirt-pin, so that the arms should not hang down. They could not carry a light, but Vincenzo remarked that the moon gave enough for all they wanted. Safely, though slowly, they arrived at the head of the great staircase, but by some accident, before they had gone down two steps, the pin got loose, one hand fell out, and, as they descended, it went flap, flap with a dead thud upon the uncarpeted oak stairs. They tried to hitch up the corpse to prevent this annoyance, but the fact of their descending position rendered this impossible.

"Vincenzo, if you don't catch up that cursed hand, I shall" (growled Roger, with a deep oath) "be obliged to drop the whole thing."

"Pazienza, eccellenza," said the impassible valet, "and don't swear. We have got the devil quite near enough to us already without bringing him any closer."

Vincenzo rested the head and shoulders of the dead body against his knees, and managing to confine the limp and drooping limb, they continued their course.

Ah, Roger Clifford! wretched man, passing now with your hateful burden beneath the large stained-glass window of the great oak staircase. Blazoned in crimson and azure are the arms of your great ancestors, and in the centre are grouped the patron saints of your noble family, while in the midst shines the image of Him who died upon the cross; murdered and forgiving His murderers. Unheeding the faint stains of colour that the moonbeams threw upon them, on they pass; and as they pass the Image of the white Christ, and the red, five sacred wounds, falls on each of the three, one after the other. Unheeded token!

They entered the study, and there the glare of the candles for a moment almost blinded them.

"Take it at once to the mouth of the well, Vincenzo. Let me have done with it," whispered Roger.

Vincenzo did so, but said:

"Eccellenza had better search his pockets first. They may contain something of importance."

"Do it," said Roger.

A bitter smile crossed Vincenzo's face, but he obeyed without a word. There was nothing of consequence in the pockets except the name of the vessel in which

Bethune was to have sailed, and of her captain.

"Keep that yourself," said Roger. "It will serve you as credentials to prove you come from him."

Vincenzo leaped down through the hole he had cut in the floor, and stooped down in a half-sitting posture at the brink of the well, from the round opening of which he had previously raised an iron plate with a ring in the centre, which had covered the mouth of the well.

"Now, sir, push the body down, the head first; I will guide it, and it will soon be over."

Roger did so, and the dark object in another minute disappeared. They listened: four times—six times—it struck against the side of the well, and then there was a faint splash, and all was silent. Quickly Vincenzo sprang back into the room. The clock struck half-past three.

"Now, sir, examine quickly his luggage, that you may see what it will be safe to send after him."

" First," said Roger, " there is this pocket-book. It is not safe to keep it, for his name is engraved in full on the gold clasp."

" Fling it in then."

They quickly looked over the rest of his things. Vincenzo was sure he could safely dispose of most of them.

He had ways and means, he said, of getting rid of them. The pistols he would be glad of for his own journey.

The rest was thrown into the well, and then, gradually, Vincenzo began pushing the iron lid into the socket in the masonry at the brim of the well. It slipped in with a heavy, loud bang, which seemed repeated and re-echoed from the depths below. A second time Vincenzo came up out of the hole, and then looking round on the boards that had been wrenched and sawn asunder, he said to Roger :

" There is now no time to lose, I ought to be off, or soon the stablemen will be stirring."

" Yes," said Roger ; " you go and harness the mare. I will do the best I can with the carpentering work, and cover it all up. And at some future period, when you and I are alone together, we must see to making it all safe."

Vincenzo went to the stables, and presently Roger Clifford heard the sound of the carriage driven to the front door. He ran out and held the mare, while Vincenzo re-entered the study to fetch what he was to take of the dead man's luggage. He flung it into the trap. The wretched Roger caught his servant's hand :

" Vincenzo, I can never forget this. You have saved me !"

"Say nothing about it, eccellenza; keep yourself well and calm, I shall be back soon."

Another moment and Roger was listening to the fast-retreating steps of the horse, and closing the front door, he returned to his study alone.

Alone with his crime and his remorse; alone with that still gaping hole that bore witness of that night's dark deed ! With rapid and trembling hands, the wretched man nailed down the boards sufficiently for present safety; he drew back the carpet, replaced the desk, and put back the large folios that had made it so heavy. For safety's sake, and to render its being accidentally moved from the spot in the floor he was so anxious it should cover, more difficult, he piled other books upon the shelves. All this required time, and the eastern sky was streaked with light before he had satisfactorily accomplished his task. He then resolved to retire to his room; and to rest if not to sleep—when would he sleep again? —till the household were stirring. He reflected, however, that first, it would be wise to look into the murdered man's room, to make sure that in their haste they had left nothing that could excite suspicion. He opened the shutters and let in the morning light. He shuddered as he approached the sofa where his victim had lain. No! there was no blood, nothing but the impression on the cushion made by the sleeping man's head. He would not shake up the cushion. He would leave it just as it was, that Nancy might, when she came in to do the room, find all the natural traces of Bethune's occupation, and of his early departure. For the same reason he left untouched the bottle and the broken egg-shells. How ghastly it all looked in that pale yellow light!—that light without warmth of a cold September morning—how his eyelids ached and smarted; how his wearied muscles wanted rest, and his strained nerves longed for sleep!

Two things had been forgotten — the evening boots, and the handkerchief Bethune was to have put on before leaving. He took them both away with him. He threw the handkerchief and boots both on the fire. It took a long time to consume these last, and he began to regret he had not hidden them; for the smoking curling leather made a bad smell, and he had to open the window to let it out. At length these miserable details were disposed of, and Roger crept, cold and miserable, to his own room.

Vincenzo had driven briskly down the

road. As he neared the lodge gate, the
gate-keeper, roused from his dreams, said to
his respected partner at his side :

"I say, dame, the devil rides to-night.
I am sure I hear Bucklyn Shaig a-coming
down the road."

Mrs. Sadler sat up in bed and listened.

" Why you be a silly one, mon. Don't
ye hear the sound of wheels? That aire
chap that I don' like to name, he rides a
hossback and not in a trap. I'm a thinking
as you will have to get up and open the
gate for the genlemon."

" Lor' a mercy on us, Betsy, I hope not.
I'll just look out a winder and see what's
a-coming."

He accompanied the action to the word,
and peeped behind the thin window-
curtains.

" Sure now, and I be blowed if it baint
master's own gig, and there's that civil
spoken Italian valet of his, a holding black
Susey's head, and a opening the gate his
self ; thank goodness for that."

" Oh, I knows now how that be," said

Betsy, in reply; " for when I was up at the house, to help in the laundry yesterday, they told me as how that genelman as was a stopping there, had to be off before daybreak. They say as he had a letter as said as he was wanted very particular, by the king of the French, as had sent a ship on purpose to fetch him; that's it."

" Lor', now to think as I should ha' taken a great man as the king of the French wants to speak to, for that hobgoblin, Bucklyn Shaig. Ha, ha!"

And thus satisfied, Mr. and Mrs. Sadler returned to their innocent slumbers.

CHAPTER X.

HOME BY THE LATERAN GATE.

THE benign influence of her native air, and the happiness of being again surrounded by her relations and the friends of her girl-hood, had had a beneficial effect on Lady Clifford's health. A winter in Rome and a summer in Albano had renewed in her the elasticity and power of enjoyment which were so natural to her, but which always seemed gradually to forsake her the longer she remained in England, and which gave place to a deep lassitude whenever she found herself under the pressure of any actual sorrow.

There are some impressionable natures that do not require strange and unusual griefs to work a lasting effect of sadness; and to leave traces deeper than the event seems to justify. We cannot always measure grief or joy by the exact nature of the circumstances that cause them, for the fountains of each lie in ourselves, and rise in proportion to the depths of our own heart from whence they spring.

The death of Mildred had left a deep shade on Angela's memory, and it was all the more fixed there from the fact of her having returned to the scenes where she had spent so many happy years with her sister-in-law, immediately after they had interred her beloved remains in the convent church of Bracciano. Devotedly attached to Lord Clifford, she yet found there was wanting in him that keenness of sympathy and power of appreciation which she required. Affectionate, kind, and attentive, there were whole fields of thought and feeling in his wife's mind which he never had explored, and to which he never even guessed the clue. The result of this was a great deal of mental solitude to the calm, deep soul of the Italian woman.

He had the frankness and chivalry of a high-born Englishman, but he lacked the fertility of his wife's southern imagination, and the deep-concealed power of affection that education and religion had subdued and directed, but that nothing could destroy, not even disappointment; and in many ways, though none for which Lord Clifford was personally to blame, her married life had brought disappointment. Upon the death of her sister-in-law, with whom she had shared every thought and feeling, and to whom she owed much of that training in early married days that had enabled her to remain contented and happy in a home that always retained somewhat the character of exile, and with a husband who was well as a companion, but not deep enough for a friend; she clung with the tenacity of devotion to the orphan child of her lost Mildred.

Lord Clifford had more than once shown a slight jealousy at her affection for her little niece; but this was forgotten when, about three years after, she had a child of her own. Still, though of course there was the mother's instinct for her own offspring, yet on the whole, Teresa was more the child of her heart than her own little Rose; and that although her dislike of the father had (if not habitually, yet from time to time) almost equalled her love for the dead mother.

Twice had Roger inflicted on Angela the severest wound it was possible for him to give her affections, by removing Teresa from her care; and the second time she had felt it more than the first. This was partly because Teresa being older, and very advanced for her age, had become more of a companion. Partly also because it had been done in spite of her most earnest entreaties; and last, but not least, because she felt 'she had not been seconded in her desire to retain the child with her, as much as she might have been by her rather careless, easy-going husband. It is doubtful whether Lord Clifford reasoned upon the fact himself, but possibly there still lurked in his mind some jealousy of Angela's love for the little orphan, and some displeasure that there was any object to share that love with himself and Rose.

In her friendship with the Princess Orsini she endeavoured to replace a portion of what she had lost. But in this case she gave more than she received. The character of the Frenchwoman had less reality and depth than that of her lost sister-in-law; and less intensity and warmth than her own. But still there was so much ready sympathy and quickness of response in the princess, that Angela sought her society more than that of any one : and besides this, there was the ever present hope that she would one day become a second mother to Rose.

It took some months of Italian life and home associations to efface from Angela's mind the profound impression occasioned in an indefinite way partly by the renewed loss of Teresa, and partly by her own delicate health : and the echo of which we have traced in her letters to the princess. Her spirits, and, as a consequence, her health began to flag again towards the close of the year after they had left England. The Orsinis had returned to their palace in Florence, and Rome from henceforth wore a deserted look to Angela. Her husband's renewed anxiety, and the advice of the physicians, led to the resolution of spending the winter at Naples, in the hope that the exhilarating air of that lovely city might have a rousing effect on Angela's languid and desponding state. It was just about the time that the terrible events we have described in the preceding chapter were taking place at Raymond Castle, that this change of residence was resolved on, and with renewed separation Lady Clifford's correspondence with the princess was resumed.

"Naples, October 30th.

"At length, dearest Louise, the horrors of our voyage are over. We were roused at an early hour this morning from our miserable sleeping accommodation on board the *Zephyr*, to catch our first sight of the Bay

of Naples; and somewhere in some of the
numerous white houses upon which the
rising sun was then shining, we were to find
a home for a few months. Line after line,
point after point was revealing itself beneath
the growing light of morning ; every second
fresh beauty burst upon our view, and the
warmth and life of day were spreading over
all. A thin column of white smoke was
issuing from Mount Vesuvius, that irascible
old hero among mountains who had formed
one of the gorgeous dreams of my childhood, a mixture of terror and wonder, and
whom now, at last, I saw actually before me.
My old nurse had been a native of Torre di
Grecco, and as I sat at her knee she used to
tell me strange weird stories of Mount
Vesuvius (which by the peasants was believed to be one of the mouths of hell), and
of the fears of the villagers whenever the
red flames reached a certain height, and the
streams of hot lava encroached on a certain
spot. From the city of Naples itself to the
very base of the fearful mountain, town
after town of white dwellings, like strings

of pearls, glittered in the sunshine along
the level shore and the vast plains, while on
the left the high grounds, as far as Baiæ,
are equally covered with villages and with
graceful villas, some of which are almost
washed by the sea at their base, while
others seem perched inaccessible on the top
of terraced and vine-covered cliffs."

———

"November 7th.

"We have found a home, my beloved
Louise, a home after my own heart. Would
you were here to share it with me! for you
too would call it a paradise, and would fully
appreciate the beauty I can find no words to
describe. My good kind husband has gra-
tified my inclinations at the sacrifice of his
own pleasures and convenience, and instead
of being actually in the town, we have a
villa on the Strada Nuova.

"The blue waves lap the walls of my
terrace garden. We are so close to the sea
that as I lie in bed I see no land, but seem
to be in a floating home, gazing on the
white cliffs of Sorrentc, or the rocky steeps

of Ischia. I hear the scream of the white seagulls swooping past my windows, when occasionally the tideless Mediterranean, trembling from the depths of its blue bosom, hangs out wreaths of white foam along its arching waves, and rushes on with a voice of thunder over the low rocks and up the granite side of the sea-walk, sometimes flinging a jet of spray so high that it startles me with a thrill of pleasurable fear while I sit safe in the shelter of my pretty villa. Oranges and catalpas, myrtles and pomegranates, fill my garden. A bank of prickly pears, and huge aloes, with the bend of their green leaves like the folds of a serpent, shut us out entirely from the road. It is a fortification of nature's own making, and my snake-like aloes guard me better than the dragon of the garden of the Hesperides. I defy man or beast to pass over that barrier. Even now I have roses in bloom, and violets without number. A trailing vine drops long disorderly tendrils from the veranda, and a group of thorny acacia have shed their blossoms, like gold feathers from the canary's wing, on the gravel path.

" Ah, Louise; a home like this, in a land like this, almost makes one cling to life again. The touch of life thrills me as I lie on my sofa in the window in the warm sunbeam, and see George enter with a few fresh flowers for my morning bouquet, while little Rose in her white frock comes skipping in. And, by the way, she bravely bears the heat; grandly betraying her half Italian origin, in spite of her fair hair and blue eyes. You cannot think, dear Louise, how that child is worshipped wherever she goes. The English colouring and cast of her features have a strange charm for the people here. The lazzaroni have given her her poor mother's name, which heaven knows she better deserves, and she is greeted as the angel wherever she goes.

" But, ah, Louise! how sadly I miss my darling Teresa, my faithful little companion. It has been a cruel separation. I feel I hardly deserved it at Roger's hands, for I have ever loved his child; and when he insisted on it, surely he must have known what it cost me—almost my life. But I submit. It is well to diminish some of the ties that bind me to a life which in this brighter land, and with better health, I still feel has perhaps too strong a hold on my earthly affections. This life out of doors, which we, in common with all Naples, are now leading, suits me marvellously. I enjoy, dear Louise, the degree of familiarity it gives me with the habits of the lower orders ; and I like to watch them basking in the privileges of their glorious climate, and requiring no other roof than that of the blue sky, with sometimes a curtain of matting or canvas, to save them from the scorching down-pouring sunbeams. My poor neighbours are a light-hearted race, fond of gambling, and greatly addicted to theatres ; but nevertheless working hard when they do work. From morning till dark I can watch the men sawing and hammering, the women stitching or knitting in the street in front of their own doors. They gossip enormously, for they are always in public.

The half-naked infants fall to the care of the very old men and women who are past harder work, and who, men and women equally, mend their own clothes; while the beggars sit together and stitch up each other's rags, for it would not be wise to take them off for the operation, lest they should fall entirely to pieces; neither, seeing how few and scant they are, would it be altogether decorous. The popular places of meeting are generally the steps of some church. They are seats by day-time, and beds by day and night, for the lazzaroni. I pass an assembly of this nature every day when I go to the Villa Reale. There is a small piazza before the church, and I am besieged daily by a crowd of bronze-limbed ragged urchins, from three to ten years of age, who become clamorous for alms the instant they see me; and I own I give it in consideration of the impudent laughter of their bright eyes, and dazzling teeth, far more than from any notion of well-merited charity. Everybody begs; even the stately maiden with her well-poised pitcher on her head, and with a brow like Juno, and a round naked ankle like Diana, does not disdain to extend a supplicating palm, and, awed by her majestic mien, I dare not refuse.

"I have paused to rest in my writing, and going to the window have seen passing the funeral procession of a young child. The white pale face is turned towards the heaven which the innocent soul has just entered; for the gay and gilded coffin is uncovered. And along the sides of the car sit his former infant companions dressed in white to represent angels, and carrying flowers to sprinkle over his early grave. All life here is translated into poetry, how much more truly than that early death which is the sure birthday into life.

"Such is life in the streets of Naples, Louise. A life of many aspects and of many sounds; while the tall palaces, with their giant porticoes, look down in melancholy desolation on the scene below. The grandeur of many of these great old houses has passed away. The lofty halls are divided into the pretty tenements of a poor and crowded population, which streams, and pours, and hurries through the narrow streets; horses and foot-passengers treading the same broad-stoned, slippery pavements, while the gutter is nowhere and everywhere. Fountains splash in the hot sunlight over their green and reeking basins at the crossing of the streets, or in the open piazzas. The ragged urchin clambers up to drink, while the dark-haired matron washes her garments in the same water beside him. Mules and asses, laden with hay, and corn, and wood, trail their sweeping burdens through the unresisting crowd. Every avocation of daily life is performed in the light of an Italian sky, in the thoroughfares of a great city, while from the silent crumbling windows of those once crowded palaces hang the many-coloured raiments of a ragged population. The casements from whence the noble ladies of olden times looked out on no less crowded streets, have become the ostentatious drying-grounds of a people to whom ablutions are little known. The jabbering sounds of the Neapolitan dialect rise high above all other discordances. Words deriving their origin from French, Greek, Arabic, and Italian, suit well a people whose habits, aspect, and even character bear the trace of all three."

" DEAREST LOUISE,

" In my last letter I gave you the particulars of our life at Naples. I must now relate to you some of the excursions we have made in the neighbourhood. It was a beautiful sunny day when we went to Castel-a-Mare. The inn at which we stayed was close to the sea, and all night long I heard the plaintive, monotonous wail by which the fishermen give notice of their presence to the other boats in their neighbourhood. The moon shone brightly on the waters; the tideless wave rippled on the shingles, and nothing broke the long silence of the glorious Italian night but that rippling sound and that wailing cry. We remember most places by what we saw there, or the friends with whom we conversed, but Castle-a-Mare comes before me chiefly as associated with those two simple sounds. The moonlight and the murmuring sea, the purple skies studded with stars, seemed, as it were, condensed into an unforgotten strain of music, and I wondered for how many ages, from father to son, that wail had been caught by the fishermen of that coast, and how many wanderers like me had listened to it through a quiet but sleepless night, and then passed on with the lingering cadence still sounding through long months and years of memory. The power of association seems always to reside most in the least tangible causes. A strain of music will call up a long line of unforgotten ghosts of the past, and a fleeting perfume will do so even more vividly. These interior senses speak to the soul with greater power than outward objects, and sink deeper into the hidden recesses of our being.

"From Castel-a-Mare we went on to Sorrento. The road along the coast is certainly beautiful, but it is a beauty which

would weary me. There is nothing grand
and imposing; there is no awe mingled
with the admiration it excites. Everything looks small and crowded, and too
many objects are forced upon the sight at
once. Some one remarked it was like
ballet scenery, or as if nature had spilt all
the colours of her pallette on Naples and its
environs. The sea is like a lake, for the
opposite shore appears, from the clearness
of the atmosphere, to be within a stone's
throw. The hills and cliffs are crushed
together. It is pretty, but not grand.
Nature has been at play here, and this is
the painted toy she has made for herself.
I love better the vast undulating Campagna
of Rome, with its melting shades and sudden lights. It seems to me as if the attend-
ant angels of creation had levelled it, and
drawn its lines, seamed it with the golden
threads of the Tiber, and set it in snow-capped
hills, that the Eternal City might spring out
of its bosom, like a natural growth of those
wide boundless plains, alone in her serene
and solemn grandeur.

" The windows of our rooms in the hotel at Sorrento looked upon the sea. I could fling a pebble straight down among the rocks in the clear water a hundred feet below. The view extends to Naples and all the coast line. It seemed as if a bird might have flown across in a few moments only. I used to sit and watch the light upon the motionless sea, and trace the slow progress, half the day through, of some white lateen sail almost becalmed in the still, hot air. My bedroom opened out into an orange garden, golden suns in a heaven of green, for the trees were laden with fruit, and sprinkled with their heavily - perfumed flowers.

" I was ill and languid, and the dreamy beauty of the place woke in my mind an impression as of something I had dimly seen before, like a recollection of some former state which lay half-forgotten in my soul. The impressions of beauty are natural to us, but they are dimmed and disfigured by the dust of life's toilsome journey. Yet sometimes when sickness lays us aside to sit silent and listen to our own hearts, we find them blurred and blotted indeed, but not effaced, and then solitude and meditation awake and renew them all again."

———

" Sorrento, December 20th.

" We are about to leave this lovely place, dear Louise, to return to Naples. While the carriage is packing, I devote the few last moments of my stay to you. I have been less well lately, and I begin to think that my old malady is creeping on slowly but surely, and that no human hand can arrest its progress. I am, perhaps, wrong in giving you pain by saying this. But I feel the need of saying it to some one who knows me and cares for me, and I cannot even allude to my apprehensions to my dear husband. The only effect upon him would be to throw him into a perfect agony, which would break down my own courage, and teach me a bitterness of regret which I desire to avoid, that, to the last, if so be God's will, I may look death in the face and bid him welcome. And how could I do this if I dwelt on George's despair, and sweet Rosy's loss! At the same time I should not like them to imagine that my silence arose from my having been ignorant of my actual danger. Therefore, to you alone, dear Louise, I confide my fear and my hope. And when I am gone, tell those who loved me, that long before the summons came, I had been listening for the footsteps of heaven's messenger.

"Yesterday I took my last and only walk at Sorrento. George had driven out towards Salerno with Rose, leaving me, as they thought, quietly tucked up on the sofa with a book until their return. They had not been gone long before a feeling of restlessness seized me, and a longing desire to be out in the open air, alone and free. I was afraid of being stopped, for it is some time since I have been thought strong enough to go out, except driving, or on donkey-back. So I slipped out like a guilty thing, and only told the porter, as I left the house, that if I were inquired for, he was to say I had gone out a short distance. I found myself in a labyrinth of high walls running along the mountain's side, and interrupting the wide view I was panting to behold. At length I came to a little wooden bridge, which spanned a narrow ravine, and led me up a mountain-path to a small terrace where stood a deserted Capuchin convent. The rusty iron gate was locked; a few flowers still grew in the neglected garden. The now silent bell hung in the open belfry with no cord attached to it. The shutters were closed, and the whole place was falling into a ruin.

"I sat down on the bank opposite, where stood the large wooden cross that the sons of St. Francis always · plant before the entrance to their houses. These crosses, as you know, have not the image of the Crucified, and the cross like the house, seemed deserted. The voices of the peasants, calling to each other in the mountain-paths just above me, floated down in the quiet soft air. I gathered bright fern-leaves from the tangled roots of an old olive-tree, and creeping up a dry narrow ditch between the mountain-side and a garden-bank, I plucked the roses that fell over. Behind me was the mountain, before me the blue sea. Some little peasant children, with pale faces, and eyes like jet, came and played near me. There was life in the soft air. Life in the ringing laugh of the peasants near me—life in the round limbs and sweet faces of the little children, life in the fresh flowers in my lap; but the silent bell, and the closed, tenantless house, filled me with thoughts of death, and I prayed that the Great Deliverer, when He came, might find me as then, sitting at the foot of the cross.

" When I reached home, I found George and Rose had returned before me, and were both in the greatest anxiety, and both on the point of setting off in pursuit. Alas! for so much tenderness, so much love lavished on one who is about to leave them. And, alas! for my own weak heart that, foreseeing their sorrow, beats again with the fond love of life! And so, Louise, you will hardly wonder when I tell you, that after treasuring my roses and fern-leaves, as mementos of that day's walk and its thoughts of death, and meaning to bear them away with me, I have just now, with the waywardness of a sick woman's fancies, dropped them down from my window into the sea below, among the rocks where I had watched the fishermen catching the silvery-scaled sardines in the early morning. I would not take them with me, because they would fade. Neither would I have them to be thrown aside by others, because my own thoughts when I gathered them had made them sacred. Ah! how difficult it is to be ever of 'one mind,' not with others alone, but with one's own better self.

"Farewell, dearest Louise.

"Yours affectionately in life and death,

"ANGELA CLIFFORD."

Not many days after writing this letter, the last she ever wrote to her beloved friend, it became apparent that the climate of Naples was getting too exciting for Lady Clifford's gradually declining strength. The feverish attacks that she alludes to in her correspondence, proved more serious than she or any of her family had apprehended. It was, in fact, the blazing-up of that consuming fire that was burning with such unnatural brightness in her large deep eyes, and lighting up, from time to time, so rich a spot of colour in her usually pallid cheeks.

The approach of spring that brought new life to all nature, and to which Lord Clifford had been looking forward with fond hope, far from renovating her exhausted health, seemed. to sap her very life, and by calling forth, from time to time, a fictitious strength, drained the strength it was expected to nourish.

Her restlessness increased from day to day, and her medical man so far acquiesced in her desire for change, that he said the soft air of Rome would, in a measure, allay the feverish irritation which was mastering her energies, and hastening her end. Her own desire to return to Rome, where she had spent so much of her girlhood, increased daily. The journey was accomplished slowly, and with difficulty; and as the carriage entered Rome by the Lateran Gate, and passed within the shadow of that grandest of churches—the "Mother and Head" of all other churches — Angela laid her hand on her husband's arm, and turning on him a face full of inspiration, murmured:

" As the shadow of a great rock in a weary land, so peacefully and sweetly falls the shadow of Rome on my burning heart. And within that shadow you will let me rest, dear George, till beneath that shadow I die ?"

From Nancy at the Castle to Mrs.
Dorothy in Rome.

" Dear Mrs. Dorothy,

" Hoping you are well, I write to say we are all in a sad way at hearing nothing of her sweet ladyship, and she so ill, as master's last letter told us. That's now nigh a month ago, and it do seem strange, that there is no post come from Italy, unless it be the letters are lost in the sea.

" Master do take on now, to be sure. But, lor! for the matter of that, he has not been the same man since last Michaelmas-tide. He goes mooning about, not a bit like his old self, and he has grown ten years older in hardly so many weeks.

" There comes no company to the house now.   It's quite altered like, and the castle seems like one great dungeon.

" It is not for such a poor servant as me to repeat all I hears; but I don't mind to you, dear Mrs. Dorothy, because you have always been so kind to me, and you won't tell on me again.   But it's just as if something had gone wrong in the house ; for people seems to shun us, like.   When master had his house full, and larking and drinking a going on, oft-times till daylight, folks seemed glad enough to come.   But now we are grown steady, no one seems to like so much as to look at us. Master goes hunting very little, and when he do, William says he keeps pretty much to hisself, and some of his old friends hardly speak to him.

"I can't tell you as I knows what the secret of it all is; and besides, I don't trust them foreign posts, where, maybe, they'll be opening my letters. In course, I don't know nothing at all about it. But people do talk so. They say as that gentleman that comed here about Michaelmas, afore or after, and as I *knowed*, because I heard them, I lying awake at the time, drove away with Mr. Vincenzo, at four o'clock in the morning, never got back to France. There have been people come over to inquire about him. I suppose that's what ails master. Nothing ails Mr. Vincenzo, that's sure. I asked him one day, what had become of the gentleman—such a gentleman as he was too! such eyes and such hair, not one of your black creatures, like that Vincenzo; but fair and clean-looking, and a noble way with him—and Mr.

Vincenzo says to me, as how the gentleman must be drowned.

" Well, but what became of the ship he sailed in, was that lost? says I. ' How should I know?' says he. ' My orders were to take him to the coast, and I took him. I know no more than the child unborn, what ship he sailed in, and that's all about it.'

" Well, they do say as murder will out, and so I suppose will drowning; but that won't be till the day of judgment, when the sea gives up its dead, and I suppose by that time no one will care what became of the gentleman, though he was so noble looking.

" All I know is, it's sad times we are come to, and I do wish you were all back again. They say when the rats run away from a house, it is a sure sign it is going to tumble down, or be burnt down. I don't know what it may be when the peacocks go. But it is as true as can be, that last Michaelmas, all those beautiful birds that our Mrs. Clifford used to be so fond of, and fed with her own hands out on the terrace, as I have heard the old servants say and as you have told me yourself, many a time, have all gone away. They must have gone in the night, for they were seen in the afternoon as usual here, and the next morning if they were not found all roosting in the cedars of Nutley Hall! and nothing has ever been able to tempt them back again.

"Master seemed much put out about it. William do say, that he never saw Mr. Clifford so vexed about a thing of the kind. I suppose it made him think of his dead wife.

"Father Netherby has been away for more than six weeks, and is only lately come back. He told me last Sunday he wanted to see Mr. Clifford; but you know master don't care much for the reverend father's company, though he is always very civil when they do meet.

"There is no news to tell you of the neighbours, that I knows of, except that young Mr. Cecil Redcliffe came of age last month, and they had grand doings up at the Manor Grange. But master did not go.

" Do write when you can, dear Mrs. Dorothy, and tell me you are coming home. It would be quite another place if you were here, and Miss Teresa had left her convent, . and were at the head of her father's house, as she ought to be.

" Your affectionate friend,

" NANCY."

FROM THE REV. FATHER NETHERBY AT NUTLEY TO LORD CLIFFORD IN ROME.

" Your lordship will appreciate better than I can express, the profound grief with which I received the intelligence given in your last letter, of your sweet lady's declining health. The sorrow, which it appears but too manifest is about to fall on you, is one far beyond the reach of human consolation; but it is not, my lord, beyond the reach of divine faith and holy hope. The distance that separates us is too great for me to say more, for I know not in the midst of what scenes of anxiety my letter may fall. Your name is ever in my prayers, and that of her whom I have loved as my own spiritual child, while I have ever admired in her the model of all Christian virtues.

" May the peace of God descend on you both, and on the darling child heaven has given you. I am greatly in need at the present time of your lordship's advice and opinion on a matter nearly relating to the welfare of your illustrious family ; and the urgency of which makes me tenfold regret your inopportune absence.

" Evil-minded and evil-designing persons have set on foot some strange stories respecting your lordship's honoured brother, Mr. Roger. And the foul calumnies that circulate, like the infection of disease in the very air around us, are the more difficult to put down, from the fact that they are so vague and indefinite, that the cunningest mind can hardly decipher their purport.

" Your lordship will perhaps question my own wisdom in alluding to such idle gossip, when I am not able to give any good explanation of my meaning. And, indeed, I have mused for many weeks on the question before I resolved to come before you with such uncertain tidings, which might reasonably lead you to doubt the saneness of my judgment. But the name of Clifford is too dear to me for me any longer to hold my peace, and I have at length brought myself to the point of writing to you on this painful subject.

"In brief then, my lord, you must know that so foolish and unheard-of a prejudice has got abroad respecting Mr. Roger, that many of the noblemen and gentry of the neighbourhood endeavour to avoid his presence. You will naturally, my lord, inquire what can be the cause of this strange state of things, and since I am not able to enlighten you on that question, my laying the subject before you may almost seem an impertinence. But your lordship knows too well my sincere attachment to your noble and pious family, to believe I am influenced by any motives but those of zeal for your honour. I might, it is true, wish that all members of your family were more like yourself, and the ways and the customs of the castle took more after those of the hall. But whatever my feelings on that matter may be as a priest, and as a friend of the family, I cannot hear the tongue of slander let loose upon the name of Clifford without indignation and astonishment. That your brother may allow himself an undesirable liberty in the matter of card-playing and dice, may be perfectly true ; but that the mere fact of a gentleman having come from France and spent a few days at the castle, and having, as the domestics assure me, left at an early hour to return to the coast and from thence regain his home in Paris, should by some strange mischance not have reached his destination—that this fact, I say, in which there may be more of the providence of God than of the malice of men, should lend any colour to injurious aspersions on the character of Mr. Roger Clifford, appears to me little less than monstrous.

" And now, my lord, you know the

subject matter of my letter, and you will understand my object when I say, return, my lord, to your own country, to your own home, and your family; that again sheltered by your honourable presence, the foul birds of slander may be scared away, and that our enemies, whom your lordship knows to be many and powerful, may cease to flout the venerable name of Clifford, and the sacred cause to which it has ever been allied.

"Praying that the blessing of God may ever descend on you and all belonging to your house,

"I remain, my lord,

"Your faithful servant in Christ,

"F. NETHERBY, S. J."

LORD CLIFFORD TO MR. ROGER CLIFFORD
AT RAYMOND CASTLE.

"Villa Negroni, Rome.

"MY DEAR ROGER,

"THE scene of anxiety and affliction from the midst of which I am writing to

you, will at once account for my writing
but seldom, and for my present letter not
half expressing to you all I might say.

"I can no longer shut my eyes to the
fact, so terrible in itself, and so agonizing in
its life-long consequences, that my beloved
wife is rapidly sinking under the effects of
that insidious malady which has already so
often threatened her precious life, and compelled me to bring her back to Italy. It
is not to you, Roger, that I need dwell on
my own feelings in this case, even were it
in my power to express them. I ought
long ago to have known that I was to lose
my dearest earthly treasure, and that it is
a marvel of heaven's mercy that I have
been allowed to detain her so long. But
even now that I see the pale shadow of
death hovering over her, and that I know
his step is on my door, I cannot realise that
I am to lose her, and less still what I am to
do without her.

"I should hardly have summoned courage to write to you now, Roger, were it
not that (without entering into needless

explanations, for you will understand my meaning if my words are to the point) there comes a time in most men's lives when they specially need the helping hand of a friend, and the support of a loyal affection. The best and noblest may be assailed by the vilest calumny, and it is just they who will feel it the most. The low underwood feels not the blast that breaks the tops of the forest trees. Keep a brave heart, Roger, and scorn the insults of the crowd. It will not be long, alas! ere the dear ties that keep me here are torn and broken, and then I shall drag what is left of my blighted life back to my own home.

" You never can have doubted, Roger, my brotherly affection, and my more than brotherly trust in you. The difference in our characters has increased rather than diminished my affectionate regard. I know I am not your equal in acquirements, or in natural talents. But fortune has made me your elder brother, and so far as that fact gives me the power of standing by you through thick and thin, and going through the length and breadth of the world with your hand in mine, you may count on all that one man, and that man a brother, can do for another.

"I shall need your sympathy when I come back to my desolate home, and I shall need your constant society, and I hope then you will find that two are better than one. You may wonder what I have heard, and I cannot speak plainer. Indeed, all I have heard is simply so vague a rumour that you may be exposed to annoyance from evil tongues, that it is impossible for me to form any definite notion myself of what has past, or is passing. Therefore, all I can say may be summed up in a hasty assurance of my faith in you, and undeviating affection. Command me in any way you please that may benefit you. And when we meet again we may defy the world!

"One word more : if you will take my advice you will fetch Teresa home; she is old enough to be a companion, and to give the charm and guarantee of a daughter's presence to your home. Lose no time about this. Angela calls me, therefore I conclude in haste.

" Your ever affectionate brother,

" CLIFFORD."

CHAPTER XI.

THE SKELETON IN THE CUPBOARD.

ROGER lost no time in taking his brother's advice with regard to Teresa. It seemed as if he had been waiting for some impulse from without to rouse him, partially at least, from the state of despondency into which he had fallen immediately after the dreadful act described in our former chapter, and in which he had been so active an accomplice. It is more than probable that had he been hardened enough in wickedness to carry things with a high hand, and brave the vague reports and dark rumours that spread through the neighbourhood, he would have at once triumphed over them.

Roger Clifford, with his noble name, his great accomplishments, and the polished charm of his manners, possessed too of a property which, though not large, enabled him to entertain his friends and prove an agreeable and useful neighbour, was not one of those on whose neck the world is in haste to lay an indignant foot. That great potentate, the world, is cautious against whom she points the finger of scorn, and she waits to hear it well confirmed that the wretch " has no friends," before she raises the cry of " hit him hard."

But Roger, in spite of his dark passions and reckless ambition, was not altogether bad; and consequently, was wanting in the desperate courage that utter depravity sometimes imparts. He could help to bury the man he had not dared to murder; and now he sat down in his gloomy castle, alone with his terrible secret, and wanting in the audacity requisite for carrying out his own game. He shrank away from those whose gaze, had he been a worse man, he ought to have braved; and growing more and more moody and abstracted, he shut himself up with his foreign books, and even seemed to think in no language but that of Italian, which was almost more familiar to him than his own. When he left the house, it was generally for a long, and apparently objectless ride, alone, over the wide, sweeping downs that lie between Nutley and the coast; or in the deep back-woods that clothe their base.

His moody habits, however, did not lead to his neglecting the superintendence of his own or his brother's property. He looked minutely into all these questions for himself, and though not naturally so fond of country pursuits as his brother he was a far more able man of business, and, as the bailiff remarked, was " 'cuter far nor his lordship, and would see through a stone wall where the other would not peep over a hedge." He was a much better man of business than one whose tastes are chiefly literary is generally expected to be. He was minute and accurate in his investigations, and severe in his exactions, but never unjust, and thus he made himself respected by the farmers and his own dependants, but not beloved. It was exactly the reverse with Lord Clifford, who was too indulgent a landlord to press eagerly and strenuously his own interests in any case where the opposite party might have, not unjustly, to suffer; and in any question of opposing rights his lordship's claims were sure to be withdrawn in favour of his weaker opponent. In many instances this system had been carried too far, and had led to abuses which had diminished the value of the Clifford property. The power of supervision could not have been thrown into better hands than those of Roger. Fond as he had been of play he had never cheated at cards, like the wretched man who had been his unhappy victim; in short, he had remained a man of honour, as re-garded money transactions, although he had been a murderer in will, and an accom-plice before and after the fearful act.

Under his care the property of his brother, as well as his own, was rapidly improving, but the improvements had not been made without exciting a certain degree of vindictiveness in many an idle farmer or dishonest tradesman, who suddenly found himself, in one instance served with a notice to quit, and in the other called to account for adulterated goods or inaccurate accounts.

It is impossible to rectify abuses without making enemies, and this was Roger's case. Of course it had been well known that high play was permitted and encouraged at the castle. Many of the gentry in the neighbourhood had learned this to their cost, and as the servants had been perfectly aware of how Roger and Henry Bethune spent their time when they were not innocently killing partridges, the rumour that the latter had never reached Paris, the gossip of the servants and the discontent of the dependants on the estate had given a handle to vague and unpleasant surmises, to which, probably, those who first uttered them attached but small importance at the time, but which grew gradually but surely into indefinite and very injurious suspicions respecting Roger.

On the morning of the day when Roger was expecting his little daughter, the bailiff from Nutley Hall called to ask whether Mr. Clifford would come and see some fences dividing the two estates, and which had been repaired by his order. Roger had sat long that morning over his solitary breakfast, and had wandered into all the rooms on the ground floor in a restless, uncertain way, as if he were examining whether everything was in order, and as if he were expecting the arrival of a far more important personage than his own daughter. Vincenzo had looked half over the house before he could find his master, and when he did so he did not fail to observe the pre-occupation of Roger's manner.

Vincenzo delivered the message from the bailiff, and asked what were Mr. Clifford's orders.

" Tell him," replied Roger, " that I am not going out this morning. I will walk over and see the fences to-morrow, and then———. Vincenzo!" he called, as the servant half-closed the door, under the impression his master had finished giving his orders. Vincenzo re-appeared in the room, and Roger, abruptly turning his back as he spoke, continued, " When you have discharged the man, meet me in the study, and bring a large tray on which I can pile up some books. I want them moved into this room, and I intend to lock up the study. You will find me there when you have dismissed the bailiff."

Vincenzo, of course, made no reply beyond a simple acquiescence, but he grew a shade paler as his master spoke, for he perceived by his voice and manner that there was something in his mind beyond the simple question of removing a few books.

When Vincenzo returned he found Roger selecting books from the shelves in the study, taking manuscripts and papers from the drawers, and altogether arranging the room as if he were gathering together everything in it he would be likely to want, and so did not intend to occupy it again. The books and papers were conveyed into the small drawing-room at the end of the long gallery, and book-cases were fetched from other parts of the house to receive them, so that at the end of less than an hour the drawing-room was metamorphosed into the study of a learned man, for with Roger a study really meant a room in which he prosecuted his varied and serious pursuits, and not a receptacle for old accounts, game books, odd numbers of magazines, cedar boxes full of cigars, parliamentary papers, and such-like more or less important articles which generally form the paraphernalia of the comfortable dens dignified, nobody knows why, with the appellation of " the study."

Silently and rapidly the two men, master and servant, did their work. Roger was paler than usual ; his brow was knit and his thin lips compressed. He stood upon the library steps handing down from the top shelves the numerous volumes of a duodecimo edition of the Italian classics. They were books that had travelled with him far and wide, hid away in his pockets, familiar friends, well worn, but well kept, and the very sight of which, and the perfume of their Russian leather binding, carried him in imagination to very different scenes, when he was young—when he was, at least, less guilty; when, in short, he had not a conscience branded by a great and dark crime. Vincenzo, too, knew well the little volumes, and, safe in the familiarity to which his master had become accustomed by so frequently having foreign servants, he broke the long silence at the moment his master handed him a well-worn copy of Boccaccio that had divided the days with Dante through a long spring and summer in beautiful Florence, some ten years previous. Vincenzo twisted the well-remembered book in his fingers, and said :

" Your excellenza should go back to where we were when I had orders always to put this book out on the dressing-table. Florence is better than England. I wish we were there."

Now, for a long time past Roger had been feeling that the presence of Vincenzo was a constant annoyance. He hated to see the man, the very sight of whom reminded him of his dreadful crime; and yet he dared not quarrel with him, or even suggest that he should leave. Again and again had he made him presents upon some excuse or other, and Roger was perfectly aware that Vincenzo found means to pay himself by peculation in every branch of responsibility which came within his scope in the household arrangements; but it was all taken by the rapacious thief as hush-money. Roger was powerless to resist. By degrees the man had contrived to take upon himself a variety of offices which had no sort of natural connection with his duties as valet, nor indeed with those of butler, a post from which he had managed to oust the former old servant who had lived at the castle, and which he had persuaded his master to let him fill, with of course, an increase of salary. In short, it had ended in Vincenzo being the master spirit of the house. Nothing was ordered for household consumption save through him, with the exception of a few things which he had found it impossible, on any pretence whatever, to take out of the housekeeper's hands. No one knew so well as Vincenzo from whence came the cognac and the French wines that were consumed at his master's table, for he managed, under one disguise or another, to be himself Mr. Clifford's wine-merchant in that particular branch; and our readers do not need to be told how readily Vincenzo could obtain these articles at a low price and sell them to Mr. Clifford for nearly as much again. There was thus every inducement to make Vincenzo anxious to remain, while the distinct knowledge that an endless and most intricate system of peculation was being carried on in his own house by the astute rascal whom he dared not accuse of it, was about as galling a punishment as could possibly have been found for the proud nature and exact, accurate habits of supervision, for which Roger was remarkable. It was, moreover, a punishment that allowed of no respite, and forbade all attempt at investigation.

Again and again, when Roger had had

brought before his notice some nefarious act of dishonesty on the part of the man he was compelled to trust, and who was constantly in attendance upon himself, his spirit had writhed at the hated bondage which kept him silent. The words that would have led to an open rupture between the two men literally burnt upon his tongue, and he would bite his lips until the blood started, in the agony of being unable to speak his mind. He would have given ten years of his life and half his fortune to have been able for once, only once, in safety to have had it out with him. He would picture to himself what he should say if by any accident he could find himself alone with the man that dogged his path, and was like the shadow of his own evil conscience, alone in a forest in the New World, alone in the desert, anywhere out of the reach of social laws and conventionalities, anywhere that he could have met him, not as master to servant, but as man to man, and then and there have told him how he loathed him ; have cursed him as his tempter

and his accomplice, have made him understand that his villany had never for a
moment been unknown to him, that he had
seen and knew, intimately knew, every
lying, thieving transaction with which he
had thought to cheat his master, and that
now and for ever he hated him, abhorred
him, renounced him! And then, if they
could only wrestle it out, hand to hand,
foot to foot. If only once his clenched fist
might fall on that villain's face, if only once
he could put his foot on him, he would not
care if the end of the struggle had left him
vanquished, so long as once, once only, he
might speak his mind aloud and strike out
like a man.

It was dreadful to walk about his own
house, feeling that master as he was of all
around him, there was one miserable wretch
who might steal and pilfer, and act uniformly in a dishonest and scandalous way,
and that he could not complain, no, nor
even glance, a look of displeasure. And
yet there was that about the man which
sometimes made Roger almost doubt whether

he were himself fully aware of the advantage he had over his master. Submissive, subservient, attentive, and oily, no word ever escaped him that even bordered upon impertinence. Sometimes, when the deep, silent hate which Roger carried in his bosom would, in spite of himself, bubble up into a few angry words, generally called forth not at all by really one of the bad deeds of his servant (for then he was on his guard, and was reminded by the greatness of the fault of his own inability to complain), but by some accidental and unintentional neglect or mistake, he would suddenly stop, and be again silent and patient by thinking he saw the sallow face grow a shade more sallow, and the deep-sunk, dark eye twinkle with a slight glitter of malignity. But, on the whole, the Italian was so uniformly and obsequiously attentive, so all-devoted to his master's wishes, so observant of his wants, and so mindful of his tastes and ways, that it was as impossible to blame him for little things as it would have been dangerous to take notice of actual dishonesty.

All that the unhappy Roger could do, hampered as he was by his own guilty conscience, was to resolve that if ever Vincenzo gave him the slightest loophole for hoping he might be induced to quit his service, he would instantly close with it. He would make it worth his while to go, if only anything he could give would induce him to leave the house and the country. But hitherto Vincenzo had uttered no word that could possibly be construed into a wish for change; and Roger could only conclude that his present position was far too profitable a one to be lightly relinquished.

When, however, Roger's eager ear caught those words, " Florence is better than England; I wish we were there," he felt his heart stop with the vehement hope that possibly the familiar fiend might be induced to leave him. For a second he dared not speak lest his voice should betray him. Still turning his face to the book-shelves, to conceal the red flush which had covered his brow, as the blood that had for a moment been held fast in his heart burst through his veins and set his pulses rapidly beating, he said, in a quiet tone, "If you prefer Florence to England, Vincenzo, you can go there when you please. You have served me a long time in this, to you foreign, land, and I would never hinder your return, but rather forward it, whenever you wish it."

There was a pause, and Roger's heart again ceased to beat. At length, as Roger descended the steps, and stood face to face with his servant, the latter replied:

"Florence is not my home, sir. I should be a stranger there as I am here, and therefore may as well stop where I am."

"I know," replied Roger, "that Genoa is your native place, but it comes to the same thing. If you wish to return there, I should be very sorry to detain you here, and indeed——"

But Roger was stopped by Vincenzo saying, slowly and with emphasis:

"Your eccellenza is very good. When you have done with my services, you have only to say so; till then I have no wish to leave this country."

As he said these words, he stepped backwards, still looking at Roger, and as he passed towards the door, he laid one hand on the large desk that stood over the fatal spot so well known to both, and without once moving his eyes from his master's face said:

"Does your eccellenza require any of *these* books to be removed?"

He could not have said more or done more to make his meaning plain. Roger turned ghastly pale, and staggered. He replied that he wanted no more books, that he had removed all he required, and the stealthy Italian, bowing respectfully, glided noiselessly from the room, closing the door after him, and leaving his wretched master alone to his reflections. And terrible indeed they were. With clenched hands and brow damp with agony, Roger paced the room, grinding his teeth, and inwardly cursing his own destiny and the fiend who governed it.

That morning, the first for many a long day, gentler feelings had stolen into his heart. The thought of Teresa's return, a vague hope that the presence of his lovely and innocent child might bring some balm to his troubled soul; a dreamy, tender, remorseful regret about the young mother of his child, whom he had not rendered happy, and whom he had laid in an early grave, little mourned at the time, but now looming in the twilight of his sad memories, together with other lost joys, lost hopes, and wasted opportunities. All this had come before him that bright spring morning, with more of tender emotion and less of bitterness than he was used to; and Teresa's arrival seemed like a ray of sunshine lighting up the gloom of his heart and opening the possibility of a calmer and better future. While thus musing, he had remembered, with the same sudden pang that was always new though it was always there, the horror that was connected with the room called his study. He fancied his child skipping across that tainted floor, perhaps some day playfully endeavouring to push aside the heavy reading-desk, perhaps recalling to him some vague recollection of having heard in her childhood that there was an old well beneath the flooring. And as these ghastly images crowded on his brain and excited his imagination, he formed the resolution which we have watched him carrying out, of moving the volumes he was most likely to read into another room, and keeping the study locked up.

There is a freemasonry of thought among the wicked, as there is the communion of saints among the good, and no doubt Vincenzo had fully read and fully understood his master's meaning. It was an opportunity not to be lost, and he seized it to rivet the chain afresh, and to show his victim that the bonds of sin are not so soon to be shaken off, and that let him struggle as he would, and grope after a better future as he might, the past still remained, and, owing to that past, neither could get rid of the other, except by a mutual understanding. There was no remorse in Vincenzo's nature. The time with him was passed for that. The devil rewards his best votaries so far in this life as sometimes to blind them completely, and to leave such callous insensibility in their souls that vice loses all its bitterness, and conscience all its sting; and in their place there is the drowsiness of a brutalised nature, the chuckle of guilty success, and the eagerness of triumphant sin.

As Vincenzo closed the door on Roger, the two men presented a strange contrast. Agony, remorse, horror depicted on the countenance of the one, and a cold, [self-congratulatory smile on that of the other. "I have him fast," said he to himself. "Does he think I have got all my reward out of him yet? No, no, eccellenza; a good murder that saved you from ruin deserves more than that. I am not going home to my old jeweller's shop in Genoa till I have lined my pockets with a great many more of your good English guineas. It is true you have raised my wages, made me presents, and the dead man's effects sold for a pretty sum, but I value the risking my neck at a higher figure than I have yet touched; and your sneaking remorse and miserable fears must make you bleed a little more before you can send your faithful servant across the Mediterranean, and so comfortably be rid of him.

The smirk grew to a laugh as Vincenzo entered the servant's hall; and he startled Nancy, who had come to fetch something, by chucking her under the chin in a familiar manner which she deeply resented, and that only made him laugh the more.

Meanwhile the unhappy Roger was pacing the room in an excited manner, maddened by the feeling that, do what he would, he could not be rid of the witness and partner of his crime. If Vincenzo could have been dismissed, there seemed some hope that the pangs of remorse would soften with time; at least his memory of the past might mellow with revolving years. Or, perhaps —who can say ?—perhaps he might one day change the despair of remorse into the soft

feelings of contrition, and die at last peni-
tent, and pardoned by God though never by
man. With this half-shadowy thought came
back the lost image of his gentle wife, and
the paternal hopes linked with the existence
of Teresa. Neglected in her lifetime, and
hardly valued, save as a pretty appendage
to himself and as adorning his house, the
memory of Mildred, buried far-off in a
distant land, came back to him full of
regret, full of pensive sadness. He thought
how, in those younger days, he had turned
from all the real happiness that lay at his
very feet, and rushed after excitement,
change, and adventure. He had worn out
the love of the sweet companion who would
have been his good angel, until she had
learnt to long for the grave into which she
had descended so early; and now what
would he not have given for one year, nay
one month, of her dear presence again?

The dissipation of Roger's past life had
not been simply the wild careless pleasure-
hunting of hot youth. It had been deeper,
more concentrated, more intellectual, and,

therefore, perhaps more guilty.   There had been as much contrast between the evil doings of Roger Clifford and Henry Bethune as there had been between the external appearance and manners of the two men. Roger had coldly and calmly succeeded in breaking the heart of the lovely girl he had made his wife, by systematic neglect far more than by giving her any real cause for jealousy.   Had she been jealous, it would have been more of his abstracted studies, his unflinching ambition, and his constant and unremitting hunt after gold, than of any attraction exercised over him by others of her own sex.

Henry Bethune had been gay, lively, false, and a swindler. Roger was cold, serious, grasping, but honourable; and possibly he would at any time have found it easier to consent to the murder of his enemy and help to bury him, as we have seen him do, than to cheat and swindle him with a smiling face and a bland smile like Henry Bethune.

As Roger, subsiding from the violent

emotion he had suffered, sat gloomily musing in the arm-chair of his study that he
was so soon to lock up and leave as a con-
demned room in the house, he dwelt with
increasing horror upon the thought that
Teresa would be dwelling with the man
he hated. His blood curdled at the idea
that his innocent child would be waited
upon by the servant who knew of her father's
guilt, who had instigated it and assisted in
it. Had it been possible it would have been
an alleviation at least to have given Vincenzo
some position that would have taken him
out of the house, such as that of bailiff; but
his being a foreigner put this quite out of
the question, and he felt more keenly than
ever that nothing but Vincenzo's own wish
could ever rid him of his presence.

He did not, of course, even in his most
nervously-excited state, apprehend by any
chance that Teresa could receive so much as
a hint of the state of the case. She at least
would be protected against that. But he
had not the same security with regard to
his son. Robert had been at home for some

time during the summer after the departure
of Lord Clifford, and consequently some
months before the murder. Roger had had
plenty of opportunity of noticing the fatal
effects of the education he had given his
son. He had perceived that Vincenzo paid
great court to the young heir, and Robert,
who, in his earlier days had, as we have
seen, been too often placed almost under
Vincenzo's care, seemed to have an affection
for the servant which for every reason was
most undesirable.

There, then, was another anxiety. Robert
would soon be coming home, and this time it
was to remain. Having no profession, his
father knew the only thing to do with him
was to let him live at the Castle, and begin
to take some active interest in the estate;
though how far he was adapted for that
kind of life, and how far his father's close
and jealous temper would admit of his
being anything more than an idler about
the place, was still a very doubtful question.
Roger had been simply and entirely glad
when Robert, weary of the dull country

and of such society as was to be found at
the castle, had asked leave to resume for
another year his wandering life. There
was but little love lost between father and
son; for having very much the same faults,
they were sure to clash perpetually; and to
the same faults Robert added much more
recklessness than had ever, even in his
youngest days, marked his father's character. In short he was at once more of a
villain and less of a gentleman. And yet
if only Robert could be induced to live at
home, and in no marked way outrage de-
corum and morality, Roger felt that his
son's presence, as well as that of Teresa,
would be a guarantee to himself; and that,
with his two children by his side, he might
get up his spirits and his courage sufficiently
to try and shake off the appearance of
gloom and the habits of solitude which, far
more than any rumours connected with
Henry Bethune's disappearance, had done
him harm in the opinions of his neighbours.

When Roger had received Lord Clifford's
letter urging the speedy return of Teresa,

he had answered it in a way to elude all direct reference to the cause of his unpopularity. He had thanked his brother for his kind zeal and interest, and had owned that in his and Angela's absence from the hall, he certainly did find his life rather solitary, adding:

"As I never think of marrying again, and no home goes on well or cheerily without the presence of a woman, I believe you are right in saying I ought to have Teresa home. The great objection to doing so is that unfortunately she is still so young that it hardly seems right to have her here without some lady older than herself; and my submitting to the presence of a governess or a companion is so utterly out of the question, that I cannot entertain the thought for a moment. However, as I did not mould my own destiny, I must just take it as I find it, and so must Teresa. I believe in the course of a few months some old friends of mine, the Count and Countess de C—— will be coming over to England; and I have written to the countess to beg she will take Teresa from the Ursuline Convent, and bring her over with them. I cannot deny that I am looking forward with more of paternal feelings than I believed I possessed to seeing the poor child again. And so thus ends most probably my intention of making a nun of her. I can only hope that she may some day find a good husband, who will be content with a pretty wife and a very small fortune. But the difficulty will be to find one. There is only one eligible Catholic match in the whole neighbourhood: of course you know I allude to the heir of the Redcliffs. And I fear that in giving her a convent education, I have destroyed my best chance of getting her to consent to a mixed marriage, even were a Protestant young gentleman to present himself."

The rest of the letter gave a detailed account of some of the important reforms that Roger had effected on his brother's estate, and of how in doing so he had necessarily made many enemies amongst the lower classes, and that they would give a great deal to be able to show their spite ; thereby adroitly insinuating that anything disagreeable that might have reached Lord Clifford's ears took its rise solely from the zealous efforts he had made in his brother's interest. If not the whole truth, it was at least part of the truth, and it would bind his brother to him more than ever, a result for which Roger was especially solicitous.

The day wore on, and still Roger sat in the fatal room, that was henceforth only to exist as forbidden ground in the castle, haunted with ghastly memories. It was indeed on a large scale, that cupboard with the inevitable skeleton that lies somewhere hidden in every house, and whose grim occupant stalks forth at night and rattles his bones within hearing of the individuals who know but too well what it is. Sometimes it is a traditional skeleton, and the members of the family will occasionally huddle together with closed dors, and concert with each other what can be done to keep that fatal cupboard locked, and prevent the skeleton from slipping off his nail and shocking everybody out of their propriety by walking into the banqueting-hall. Sometimes it is a private skeleton, known only to one sad inmate in that large house, and who bears his burden alone, and wrestles with his enemy in the dead of the night. But surely there are few roofs that harbour such a skeleton as that at Raymond Castle!

At length Roger roused himself to go. Sometime previous he had had a special lock put upon the two doors of this room, that he might always feel secure that no one could enter it without his permission, should he see fit to keep it locked. And so he passed out of it, and turned the key, and went back to the room he had been preparing for Teresa, and where but a few hours before he had himself been arranging some pictures and ornaments to make it more like a lady's boudoir, with almost a feeling as if there might be even for him some future possible happiness. The interview with Vincenzo had dissipated the illusion.

CHAPTER XII.

THE ANGEL OF THE HOUSE.

THE housekeeper had been sent to London to meet Teresa, and to receive her from the hands of the Countess de C——. She had left her convent some weeks previous, and had been stopping with her father's friends in Paris, in order to allow time for her to exchange the dark blue dress—a fac-simile of which she had appeared in on her arrival four years previous at Nutley Hall, and the recollection of which had so haunted her father's fastidious taste that he had written to beg she might be furnished with a complete trousseau of more worldly habiliments —before she quitted Paris. The result had been altogether satisfactory, for the

Countess de C—— understood the matter thoroughly, and had been greatly pleased with having the charge of her old friend's lovely daughter; nor had she confined her duties to buying clothes, for when she saw the effect they produced in enhancing Teresa's beauty, she had been unable to resist the temptation to carry her young protégée a little into the gay world of Paris, and she had done so with the greatest success. And so at length when the post-chaise drove up to the door, and Roger was standing at a little distance in the long gallery, and feeling a little strange but decidedly pleased, he was almost startled to see before him a very lovely girl; not like a school-child, not like a nun, but beaming with youth and bright beauty, exquisitely dressed, graceful in every movement, and with two large, glorious dark eyes looking out of a face of the most perfect oval, with a complexion of clear, dead white, lips of the deepest crimson, and teeth of faultless regularity. There was no shyness, no constraint in her manner. Father and daughter had not met for four years, and yet this beautiful creature sprang forward with open arms; the two little hands in a second were lightly placed on his shoulders, and with one little clear ringing cry of · "My dear father!" he found himself kissed on both cheeks before he had had presence of mind to move a step. He took her hands in his, and held her off a pace, not speaking, but scanning that sweet, bright face with a pleased smile. At last he said:

"Why, Teresa, I thought you were a child!"

"A child, papa? Don't you remember I am eighteen, and quite a woman now? It is so long ago since you saw me I hardly wonder you have forgotten all about me. But now, dear papa, I am coming to live with you, and keep your house, and try to make you love me, though you do know so little about me. Ah, papa, I am so glad to come home!"

The large eyes glistened for a moment brighter still from the tears of joy that filled them; and it was, perhaps, not

strange that the eyes that looked into them
were moistened also, unused as they were
to any tears, save those of bitterness.

He took her to her room, and waited
upon her in a thousand little ways to make
quite sure she had all she required. She
had brought a French maid with her not
many years older than herself, and prepared
to die of *ennui* in the gloomy castle pe-
rennially surrounded by fog—a view of the
subject to which she had made up her
mind as a matter of course.

It was a strange sensation to Roger to
find himself sitting after dinner *tête-à-tête*
with his new-found daughter. He began
to wonder why he had left himself without
her society so long, till he recollected that
his intention had been that she should enter
the religious life. That thought seemed to
him now so uncalled-for as to be quite pre-
posterous. He could not recollect why he
had ever wished it; and as he contemplated
the graceful figure before him, and watched
the little fingers busily working, the bend
of her small head, with its wealth of brown

hair, the little ear peeping out from beneath the wavy curls like a small white shell; as he watched the long lashes fall on a cheek that had caught the tint of the roseleaf, he could not conceive what had ever put it into his head to deprive himself for life of such a treasure-store of youth and charm, when he had it in his power to grace his own home with it—at least for a time. And then her voice was so melodious, it had such variety of tones, and rose and fell in such harmonious cadence that he kept asking her questions about the convent and about what she had seen and done in Paris, far more to listen to the sound than to get information. She was like her mother, but she was more truly beautiful, and he thought he perceived that she had that elasticity of mind, the want of which he had always felt in his poor wife, though the probability is that he himself had broken the spring, and then complained it did not act.

In short, it was altogether so new, so strange, and so full of promise, that Roger already began tofancy himself a better and a happier man, and for that evening even the presence of Vincenzo, and all the recollections which that inspired, were nearly lost sight of.

Before a week was over, Teresa was thoroughly installed in the castle as its mistress and good angel. She had created her position by from the first taking it for granted it was to be hers. She laid claim to her father's affections as unhesitatingly as if she had always enjoyed them. Without shyness, and yet with perfect delicacy, she had taken it for granted she was to be his companion under all circumstances where such was possible. The frankness with which she talked to him necessarily in great measure broke through his own reserve; and though he would sit with her for an hour together, seldom saying more than just enough to keep her talking, yet she felt his eyes were upon her, and that he was giving her a pleased and kindly attention.

She quickly found out that he was a great Italian scholar, and thereupon insisted upon learning the language herself, and taking him for her preceptor. At first he thought it would prove a mere caprice; but when he found long exercises brought him to correct, day after day, he saw that she was thoroughly in earnest about that as she was about everything she undertook. He soon learnt that whenever Teresa began a thing she meant to go on with it, and that, in truth, she generally managed to secure success by a mixture of perseverance and of sweetness, which no one could long resist.

There were, however, two subjects upon which she never touched with her father, and these were the two nearest her own heart—her religion and her mother's memory. Her perceptions were as true as they were delicate—and indeed they can never be the one without being the other also—and she had from the first instant perceived not only that she should meet with but little sympathy from her father on these matters, but that also there was a sternness in his manner which made her apprehensive of displeasing him by allusion to them. With regard to her mother she was too loving and innocent herself to attribute her father's silence to anything but the depth and intensity of his feelings, which rendered all reference to his lost wife only too painful. But upon the subject of religion she was seriously anxious, and felt that, so far as was consistent with her obedience and submission as a daughter, she was bound not to let the subject go by default. She had reached the castle on a Tuesday, and all that week had passed without any reference to the subject upon which all her thoughts were bent. When Sunday came, and she was dressed to walk the short distance across the park to the little chapel, she had taken it for granted she should find her father ready in the hall to accompany her. He was not there, but Vincenzo was laying out his master's hat and gloves as if he were expecting him to go out soon. She paused a moment, and then asked the servant if her father were nearly ready for mass. The man continued his occupation without raising his head, and did not reply till she repeated the question. Probably by that time he had made up his mind it would be better to tell her the whole truth at once. So he replied:

"No, signorina, my master is not ready, nor will he be. Mr. Clifford never goes to mass here."

Teresa changed colour, but immediately felt it was not a subject on which it would be possible for her to make any reply to the servant. So, recovering herself quickly, she said:

"Will you be so good as to tell my father I am gone?"

She left the house with a heavy heart. Sunday after Sunday her father missed his mass of obligation, and that entailed missing all his other religious obligations. It was awful to think of, and she must make up her mind whether she was not bound to pluck up enough courage to ask him to accompany her the following week. When she returned home, nothing was said by Mr. Clifford on the subject. He seemed to look upon it quite as a matter of course that she was to go and he was to stop away.

Teresa was resolved to do nothing in haste, lest she should spoil her sacred task by precipitation; but she was quite resolved that nothing should interfere with her own pious practices so far as she was free to continue them. And as her father did not breakfast till after nine, she had ample time, those bright summer mornings, to go to eight o'clock mass, and be back again before she could even be missed. She had many hours in the day when she was entirely left to herself, for her father was out a great deal; and even when he was in the house his habits of study were too ancient and rooted for him to break through them entirely, though certainly his books did not engross as much of his attention as before his daughter's arrival.

Teresa decided on endeavouring to obtain some more information about her father's religious, or rather anti-religious, sentiments before she uttered a word to him; and consequently a day or two after the first shock of finding he did not even go to mass, Mrs. Brown the housekeeper, who had lived in the family for years, having come to the drawing-room to speak with Teresa on domestic affairs, she thought it was better at once to ask what she wanted to know. So when dinner was ordered, and business dismissed, just as Mrs. Brown was on the point of leaving the room, she stopped her, and said, with a slight tremor in her voice:

"Mrs. Brown, I am not afraid of asking you a question which I could not put to any one in the house except yourself. You have known me since I was a child, and you knew" (and here her voice faltered, and tears came into her eyes) "my poor mother. I want you to tell me, is it true that my father never goes to mass? He did not come with me last Sunday, although there was nothing that I knew of to prevent him; and when I happened, in the hall while waiting for him, to ask Vincenzo if he were coming, he replied that he never went."

Before Mrs. Brown had opened her lips,

Teresa, saw by her countenance, that her avowal was not going to be a satisfactory one. Mrs. Brown shook her head sadly, and said :

" Indeed, miss, I grieve to say, it is too true. Mr. Clifford never goes to mass here. When his lordship is at Nutley, and my master is stopping there, he does go sometimes with the rest of the family. I suppose he feels he could hardly help himself there, for his lordship is very particular, and my lady still more so ; and Mr. Clifford is such a gentleman he would not like to annoy anybody. But you know, miss, it is not exactly being a gentleman that will make him a good Christian, and, certainly, when he is in his own house. though perhaps I ought not to say it to his daughter, he might be an infidel for all he seems to think of his religion. But there, miss, I don't want to pain you," she added, as she saw two large tears brimming over in Teresa's eyes, " only as you, miss, know what is right, and have been brought up in a Catholic country, a convent and all, we do hope, we *all* hope, miss, and Father Netherby says the same, that in time, you may bring master round, and that will be a happiness for all of us."

" And how was it, Mrs. Brown, in my poor mother's time ?"

" Oh well, miss, it wasn't as it should have been, nohow. Your mamma, miss, was an angel, and I suppose that is why she died. She was too good for this world, and too good for the fate that befell her; not but what, miss, we are all attached to Mr. Clifford in a way. He is a just master, though he is a gentleman to be afraid of. But, as I always say, if he had other people about him besides those that be about him, he would be a different gentleman altogether. It is not only ' like master like man,' Miss Teresa, it's sometimes like man like master. There is no one can abide Mr. Vincenzo ; and he, you know, has master's right ear; and when anything is done as should not be done, lor bless you, miss, it's ten to ten thousand, that that foreigneering rascal is at the bottom of it. I beg your pardon, miss, I am afraid I am saying more than I ought to do. But I would not have you think, miss, that the fault is all with your dear papa. And we are all so pleased to see how fond he grows of you. And who knows, miss, but what you are come on purpose to change the face of things? and you'll get your papa round to your way of thinking, aye, and perhaps Master Robert, too, in time; for that's a worse case still."

"Tell me, Mrs. Brown," said Teresa, in a low voice, husky with her choking tears, "Was my mother not happy with my father?"

Mrs. Brown made no verbal reply; but she looked hard at Teresa, pressed her lips very tight, shook her head very slowly, gave a great sigh, and turning to leave the room laid her hand on the door.

"Stop one moment, Mrs. Brown," said Teresa. "Can you give me—may I have the key of my dear mother's oratory? I remember it always used to be kept locked, I suppose it is so still."

Mrs. Brown replied that she would fetch

it, and left the room. When she returned, she found Teresa with traces of tears on her pale cheeks.

" Now, my dear young lady," said the motherly old woman, " you must not let what I have said make you unhappy. It is as well, perhaps, that you should know just what is before you, and what kind of a house you have come back to. And thinks I to myself, it is better the dear young heart should learn all about it from an old woman like me, as knew all the family before she was born, than go on finding it all out by degrees, and perhaps not knowing what to do, or which way to turn. With God's help, miss, you'll make all different, and that's what Father Netherby says : and he knew your blessed mother, aye, and our sweet Lady Clifford, too, who is so ill that nothing but a miracle can save her."

By this time, Teresa's tears were flowing fast, and Mrs. Brown was beginning to repent of the whole conversation. She soothed her with kind words ; she flattered her, to try and raise her courage, and she did not leave her until she heard Teresa say quite calmly that Mrs. Brown had done quite right in telling her the whole ; and that she hoped she would pray for her, that she might have the strength and the prudence necessary for the difficult position in which she was placed.

It often happens to us, that beneath the surface of our daily avocations and the routine of our life, we have a vague sense there is lying some new duty not yet realised that is waiting only for a special occasion to put it plainly before us, and make us hear that trumpet-call of conscience " Arise and walk !" Suddenly, the voice of God wakes us from our slumbers, and summons us to our new task. Shuddering at our weakness, thrilled through with the sense of a new responsibility, and yet braced with the hope of fulfilling a duty, and giving glory to God, we resolve and prepare ; and, from that hour a change has passed over the soul. It takes but a moment ; but that moment is decisive. The heart is older by years. The boy has become a man, and the dreaming girl wakes up full of purpose into the calm, serious woman. It is a shower of grace on the soul, like the showers in the natural world between a radiant morn and a hot noontide, when the warm well nurtured rosebud expands at once, and all the enclosed beauties of its crimson heart are laid open to the sun.

Teresa's feelings on returning home from her convent education, had been such as were natural to her age, tempered by the seriousness and piety of her own character. But she had not been long there before the vague sense of some grave new duty was dimly stirring in her heart. And now it all burst upon her. Raymond Castle had had no mistress for eighteen long years, and its last mistress, her own lost mother, had spent there a few years only, and those unhappy. Meanwhile, a godless man had come and gone, as his views or his pleasures had impelled him, and that man was her father; and the only other figure in the dark picture was her brother, and that, as

Mrs. Brown had said, " was a worse case still." This was her home, these were her prospects, and alone and unaided she would have to steer her course ; and what was harder, to try and guide others. For a space, it seemed to her as if the very ground were sinking beneath her. As she stood at the window, looking over the sweeping park to the long line of downs fringed with wood that bordered the horizon, it seemed to her as if a change had passed even over the external world, and a grey mist fallen upon nature. For a moment the light had gone out in her heart, and that is the light in which we see the world outside us. But by degrees, her inner sense caught the clarion sound of conscience and of duty. Like a spirit it came, breathing music ; dappling with footsteps of light the green undulations of the swelling hills ; thrilling over the forest leaves that turned trembling their paler surface to the sky ; breaking the stagnant pools into sudden smiles, and with a rush of glory flashing up the sloping park, where the dappled deer were for a moment swathed in light, and straightway falling on the grey castle walls with a flood of golden sunshine.

Utter abnegation of herself — absolute devotion to a fixed purpose, that was what Teresa saw before her, and what with intense earnestness, she adopted and embraced. She must win her father, and lead him to God: and to accomplish that, everything if needs be, must make way; no mere joy of youth lay before her; no day dreams of a future for herself. The present absorbed all, and must continue to do so each hour, as it came and ceased to be the past and was not yet the future. The present!—the present! All duty lies in that, all grace, all eternity. No schemes for future development, no dreams of vast improvement to come! The great *now* is the only reality for us, for all else hangs on it. O foolish man! crush into the present moment all thy being. Let this instant beat of thy heart be the one most vehement in love to God, most abject in penitence, most ardent in faith. This is your opportunity. This, and no other, is yours, and at the end of it hangs Eternity!

Teresa pondered much and long on the work she saw before her, and with a maturity of thought beyond her years and experience, decided that it would be impossible to attempt anything abrupt or marked towards accomplishing the task of getting deeper into her father's confidence, and so of endeavouring to obtain a permanent and beneficial influence over him. She felt it could only be done by making him love her, and being herself full of affection towards him she did not apprehend much difficulty in that. On the contrary, she felt that she had already made as much way as she could expect, and even more.

But as the question of what was to be done in the complicated incidents of home life were sure to be, from time to time, difficult and embarrassing; she resolved on taking Father Netherby—that old friend of the family, into her confidence, and determined to be guided, not only by his advice as a priest, but by his knowledge of her father, and the experience he must have acquired in his intimate relations with the whole family.

She found Father Netherby all kindness and sympathy; but at first, she was a little chilled by his apparent want of hopefulness, and she was struck by his betraying far more anxiety about herself, and giving her more paternal advice with respect to her own private conduct, than by any lively interest he seemed to take in the efforts she was so anxious to make with regard to her father. He rather seemed to shrink from the idea of coming to the castle to see her; except, perhaps, at very rare intervals, and did not at all share her innocent convictions that if only he would accept the invitations she felt so hopeful of inducing her father to send, a little more intercourse between Mr. Clifford and the priest must result in effecting all else she desired.

"You know my daughter," said Father Netherby, calmly and sadly, "it is not that Mr. Clifford is ignorant upon any point connected with the faith. Your father is, perhaps, as well read in doctrinal theology as I am, who have made it my study all my life. It is not his reason or intellect that has to be attacked, it is his heart. And that I believe and trust you may be able to touch, by constantly letting him find in you a dutiful and most affectionate daughter, showing yourself subservient to his wishes in all questions that do not affect your conscience; but firm as a rock whenever your duty happens (which God grant may never be the case) to clash with his wishes."

Teresa soon found that in her conversations with Father Netherby, she obtained always a great deal of valuable advice, while at the same time, she gathered very little information respecting facts. Father Netherby seldom made any remark which served to throw any light upon her father's character.. And though he talked to her a great deal about her mother, and had a whole store of anecdotes of her kindness to the poor, her sweetness, and her piety, yet the discourse never elicited any account of why, or in what way, Mrs. Clifford's marriage had not been a happy one. Everything was taken for granted, but nothing was explained. At first, this a little surprised and disappointed Teresa. But as time went on she felt how wise and right it was.

Teresa had heard from Father Netherby, and also from Mrs. Brown, of Lady Clifford's precarious state of health. She had asked her father about it, and he had confirmed the statement that her aunt was very ill. But as he had not dwelt upon the subject, Teresa had failed to perceive that it was not merely a question of being out of health, but one of life and death, which any moment might decide unfavourably. Teresa's affection for her aunt, who had indeed been a second mother to her, was unbounded. And though she had now not seen her for a very long time, long at least in so young a life, yet every association of affection and happiness was connected with Lady Clifford in Teresa's memory. One of the first rides she took with her father, she entreated to be taken to Nutley Hall, and when there had dismounted, and leaving her father in the library, had run all over the house, visiting the nursery and Lady Clifford's own dressing-room, and the now disused chapel; uttering aloud exclamations . of tenderness to the very walls, and smiling and weeping by turns, as countless incidents of her early childhood were recalled to her mind by the objects in the house.

She had begun her course in the highest spirits, but by the time she had revisited each nook, scanned the titles of old well-remembered story-books in their school-room, stumbled in the dark passage over Rose's rocking-horse, and found the empty cage where her pet canary had lived, she was more than subdued ; and when she returned to her father she looked pale, and had evidently been weeping. She found him absorbed in an old edition of Froissart, that he had wanted to consult, and she stood full five minutes looking through her tears out of the window upon the garden, and the shady cedars, and the haw-haw, before he even noticed her presence. When he declared himself ready to mount, she followed in silence, and through the rest of that day's ride but little was said by either party. Once or twice Roger looked furtively at the little pale face, whose delicate outline stood clear against the blue sky, as they rode along the uplands to the north of the castle. He wondered what was passing in her mind, and, evidently, the question fretted him. Her love for the home of her childhood, which was not his home, roused some of that jealousy that we have already remarked as one of the strongest of Roger's characteristics.

Her loving recollection of her uncle and aunt was a tacit reproach of his own neglect. And now that he had at last chosen to bring his daughter home, and condescended to care for her and really to love her it was only consistent with his nature that he should at once lay claim to all her affections, that he should ignore the past, and expect as much from Teresa in return for his tardily-bestowed affection, as if he had

always taught her to bask in its warmth;
but his moodiness was lost upon Teresa: she
rode silently by his side, ruminating the
past, calling to mind Lady Clifford's intense
Italian endearments, her uncle's indulgent
ways, her bright little cousin, and the sweet
harmony of domestic peace, demonstrative
affection, and unaffected piety that had per-
vaded the whole house.

The contrast between that and her own
house struck her forcibly. Certainly it was
very melancholy—a young, solitary girl,
and a moody father absorbed in his books,
or in his gloomy thoughts—fond of her, it
is true, but betraying selfishness even in his
love. Already it seemed to her a long time
since she had been living the monotonous
life of Raymond Castle, and no break had
come, no new sympathies, no fresh hopes;
at least, so it seemed to her. If we could
have heard Mrs. Brown's account of the
matter we should have found that others
were conscious of an improvement which
escaped the observation of her who had
caused it.   Mr. Clifford's domestics found

him less severe, less exacting. The neighbouring poor were astonished to find that
" up at the castle " there were certain days
when their wants were supplied, and some
of the good things in the larder and kitchen
found their way to the cottages, much as
was the case " down at the hall " when " my
lady " was at home.

Mr. Vincenzo was perhaps about the only
person who did not appreciate the difference. He found his master had become
more independent of him. One of the foot-
men had been specially deputed to wait on
Miss Teresa, and answer her sitting-room
bell; and, somehow or other, it happened
that when Mr. Clifford wanted anything he
generally contrived to go to his daughter's
room, and there ring for the servant, and
thus avoided having so much of the presence
of Vincenzo. Also, he would have his
daughter to sit with him when he was
dressing for dinner, and her presence was a
good excuse for sending the valet out of the
room to wait in the passage till he was
wanted. All this was not at all to Mr. Vin-

cenzo's mind. He sulked about it a good deal to himself, while his manner was more oily than ever to his master. Meanwhile, he endeavoured to indemnify himself for what he chose to consider Mr. Clifford's ingratitude by organizing a few more little peculations, and managing to insert his finger in numerous domestic pies that were not originally cooked for his benefit, and had nothing to do with his natural department.

When Teresa and her father entered from their drive, Teresa walked straight through the hall up-stairs without a word. As she passed along she heard Vincenzo, who had met them at the door, say to her father:

" Eccellenza, the post has come in, and there are letters from Italy." She heard the sound of the words, but they awoke no reflection, and, absorbed in thought, she went to her room to change her habit, and read till dinner-time.

LONDON: PRINTED BY WILLIAM CLOWES AND SONS, STAMFORD STREET
AND CHARING CROSS.